THE AMERICAN ENVOY

May 2010

To Brian,

Very best wishes.

GARBHAN DOWNEY

Garbhan Downey

GUILDHALL PRESS

Published in February 2010

GUILDHALL PRESS
Unit 15, Ráth Mór Business Park
Bligh's Lane
Creggan
Derry
Ireland
BT48 0LZ

T: 00 44 28 7136 4413
E: info@ghpress.com
W: www.ghpress.com

The author asserts his moral rights in this work in accordance
with the Copyright, Designs and Patents Act 1998.

Designed by Kevin Hippsley/Guildhall Press
Copyright © Garbhan Downey/Guildhall Press
www.garbhandowney.com
ISBN: 978 1 906271 27 5

This publication is available in various e-book formats
from www.ghpress.com.

A CIP record for this book is available from the British Library.

Guildhall Press gratefully acknowledges the
financial support of the Arts Council of Northern
Ireland as a principal funder under its Annual
Support for Organisations Programme.

All rights reserved. No part of this publication may be reproduced or transmitted in any
form or by any means, electronic or mechanical, including photocopy, recording, or any
information storage or retrieval system, without permission in writing from the publisher.
This book is sold subject to the condition that it shall not, by way of trade or otherwise,
be lent, resold or otherwise circulated without the publisher's prior consent in any form of
binding or cover other than that in which it is originally published and without a similar
condition to this condition being imposed on the subsequent purchaser.

Garbhan Downey has worked as a journalist, broadcaster, newspaper editor and literary editor. He spent two years as a full-time student politician after graduating from University College Galway in 1987 and was Deputy-President of the Union of Students in Ireland. His novel *Yours Confidentially: Letters of a would-be MP* was listed as one of the *Philadelphia Inquirer*'s top seven International Crime Reads of 2008. His last book, *War of the Blue Roses*, was columnist Eamonn McCann's Novel of the Year for 2009. Downey lives in Derry with his wife Una and children Fiachra and Bronagh.

Note:
This book is a work of fiction. All characters in this publication – other than those clearly in the public domain – are fictitious, and any resemblance to real persons, living or dead, is purely coincidental.

Many thanks to the Guildhall Press team of Paul Hippsley, Declan Carlin, Jenni Doherty and Joe McAllister for continuing to make this process fun and completely fret-free. A special award to Kevin Hippsley for designing so many excellent draft covers that settling on just one was ridiculously difficult. Appreciation to Peter Rozovsky of international crime-fiction blog Detectives Beyond Borders for his valuable editorial input.

Also, heartiest congratulations to GP for becoming the first Irish publishing house to produce an e-book and printed novel simultaneously.

My deep appreciation as always to my family for their love and support, and particularly to my uncle, Martin Downey, for giving *Envoy* its first 'macro'-read and suggesting some very valuable improvements.

*It is terrible to contemplate how
few politicians are hanged...*
GK Chesterton

To Cormac and Tracey
May life be ever kinder to you

PROLOGUE

How US Consul Dave Schumann ever wound up at a bump-in-the-road like Derry I'm still not quite sure. The entire island of Ireland wouldn't even add up to a decent New York borough, and here he was, setting down sticks in an outpost so remote that the next stop north is Reykjavik.

But I suppose Dave's Boston upbringing meant he'd a natural affinity with the Irish. And, of course, if he ever decided to continue in politics, a couple of years spent among the chosen people would be worth a bagful of votes, as presidents from Kennedy to O'Reagan and O'Bama can testify. So I'm sure there was some logic there somewhere.

Anyway, however it happened, we were glad to get him.

We all knew Dave would need a minder to help him read the greens for the first few weeks – and more importantly teach him who (and who not) to do business with. But the word we got back was that this man was sharp and wouldn't need prolonged and undue hand-holding, unlike most of our local politicians.

American pols tend to be like that. More intent. More focused. More professional. They have to be, as what they say invariably counts. Politics isn't a hobby to them like it is here. It's about the administration of real power – and real money. Not squabbling over pennies and cajoling your neighbours in Britain or Europe into throwing you a few crumbs on budget day.

By dint of fluke, my old man had done some business with Dave's grandfather a few years back, so I was given the job of befriending him and steering him clear of the local vermin. Men like 'Darkly' Barkley – and others who aren't so obvious.

It was further suggested that I should set up a 'safe' network for the new guy – a card school, perhaps – consisting of just a few trusted friends and/or valuable contacts. Which is where Monty Boyce, the mayor of Mountrose, came in. As a valuable contact, that is, not a friend. For all his charm, I wouldn't trust Monty as far as I could spit the jack of diamonds. He drinks too much and then blames it for his bad decisions. But I do enjoy his company, and we've been playing poker together for twenty years, on and off, even if I've never won a hand.

I was also warned, re-warned and warned again to try to regulate certain of the new Consul's weaknesses – in particular, his twin loves: good-looking women and playing investigative reporter.

Dave was a newspaper editor back in the States and never really quit the habit. Still has the nose for when something's not just right. And, as you know from the media, he is also quite the sharp-dressing bachelor. Very handsome as well – a bit too pretty, perhaps – but completely clueless when it comes to the fairer sex. (Though how that makes him different from any of the rest of us, I'm not quite sure.) So to keep manners on him, I resolved to introduce him to my bad-tempered, redheaded, ultra-feminist niece, Ellie, as soon as possible. Not soon enough, as it turns out. But more of that anon.

The one thing I never expected of Dave was that he'd keep a written record of his time in Derry. It defies everything I know about the man. In every other aspect of his life, he's so damn cautious. But then I spend my days dispensing very expensive advice to men and women who roundly ignore everything I tell them. So who am I to judge?

In hindsight, though, it's fitting that there's a full account of what happened here this spring. Even if it will be another fifty years before the Yanks let us publish it – or indeed a lot longer. After all, it's not every day that a US envoy finds himself neck deep in a litany of murder, arson, smuggling and drug-running. Or maybe it is. What would I know? I'm only a humble country lawyer.

If, however, you ever do get to read these letters, you may safely assume that everyone connected with this tale is dead, in jail, or otherwise beyond prosecution. That, or the CIA have rewritten the entire thing so convincingly that Spielberg will be looking for the movie rights.

Either way, one thing's for certain: you'll never know the difference.

Tommy 'Bowtie' McGinlay
Solicitor-at-Law
Derry, Ireland

JANUARY
♣

US Consulate
Whitman House, Derry

Dear Pop

Okay, okay, you were right. That impression of Bill Clinton was always going to get me in trouble. But how in the hell could I have predicted Hillary was going to get State – or, indeed, that Joe Biden knew how to upload his videophone onto YouTube? And no, it's no consolation that the clip of me and the cigar has now as many hits as Paris Hilton getting out of that limo.

Hillary, according to The Boss, actually wanted me sent to head up the new office in Gaza – *vey is mir!* – but Biden felt guilty at what he'd started and beat her down to Northern Ireland. His folks are from Derry (at least at election time they are), and he assured me that since the Troubles stopped fifteen years ago, it's one of the safest cities in Europe. He also promised that if I kept my nose clean I'd be back in Washington within the year – and that he was terribly sorry for the embarrassment he'd caused me. (That loud ringing noise you can hear is the fire crew on their way to put out Joe's pants.)

But whisper it quietly, Pop. Though I'm only here a week, I've already fallen in love with the place. The city itself is stunningly beautiful, more of which anon. And as for the people – by God, they're hospitable. Twenty years of alcohol awareness messages have just sailed right over their heads. But the one thing that sets both Derry and its citizens apart is their abiding certainty that this little town (population 110,000 at a push) is the center of the universe.

We're not talking opinion here, either. They don't *think* Derry is the center of the universe – not in the way that we believe DC to be – they *know* it. Forget whatever Galileo taught you. The world, the solar system and the universe all revolve around them. All life begins, ends and is centered here. Everything else is gauged solely on how it relates to Derry.

England, for example, exists solely as the country to blame for all of Derry's woes. And while the British public sector still funds two out of every three jobs here, it is only fitting that it does so – to pay for the colonial injustices of yesteryear. Derry natives – you gotta love 'em – are past masters at guilt: they could even teach Rabbi Silberman a thing or two. And the poor British have much to feel guilty about. So they've spent the past ten years cutting 'I'm Sorry' checks quicker than you did when Mom caught you with Sally the housemaid.

The Irish government (the island's main government, based in Dublin) is likewise still suffering the consequences for allowing Derry (and the other five northern counties of the island) to be partitioned off into the United Kingdom in the 1920s. Dublin's guilt is compounded by the fact that, for all their anti-British saber rattling, they'd sooner put their *shmekls* in the microwave than re-unite the country. Accordingly, they, too, tend to lower their eyes and nod their heads nervously when Derry demands a hearing. But the Irish influence, and their money, is largely notional rather than actual: they kick in squat compared to Downing Street. So in effect, they spend most of their time acting as a back-up tag-wrestler for Derry when things aren't going too well with the Brits.

America, however, is a particular friend of the city: we're pretty much regarded by all as the kindly uncle. It dates back to World War II, when the city was the largest Allied naval base in the North Atlantic, and we had a huge camp here. The GIs were great mixers and were never afraid to spend money; many of them even married locals. Their generosity, and the fact that we'd already beaten Britain in a war, made us many friends. The links, in fact, go back even further. Derry was a big emigration port for the Irish leaving for the New World in the nineteenth and early twentieth centuries. There isn't a family in the city that hasn't got a cousin somewhere on the East Coast. Then, in the 1960s, we gave them an Irish Catholic president, and Derry all but signed up to become the 51st state. No lie; there are still dozens of homes here that have pictures of Kennedy on the kitchen wall, right up alongside Pope Benedict.

If the US is Derry's favorite uncle, however, there's little doubt who, or what, is the city's evil stepmother: Belfast, the state 'capital'.

Belfast is home to the new Stormont Administration, set up to try to run this little bastard 'country' after forty, eighty or even 800 years of war – depending on what size grudge you carry. By any rational reckoning, Stormont is not a government at all. It has no tax-raising powers, no law-making powers and can be overridden at the flick of a pen by London. (Kinda like when you gave me my first motorcycle and fitted the block to make sure it couldn't go over thirty.) In effect, it's a vastly overstaffed committee that carves up a regional budget. But it still manages to piss off Derry no end by ensuring that what little money and industry there is stays in and around Belfast. (By the way, if you ever want to start a fight in Derry, just refer to Belfast as the capital, without any ironic inflection. They'll hang you from the Guildhall clock.)

The Derry pols do the best they can, but there is an age-old Belfast reluctance to pump any money west of the River Bann (check the map) just in case the Southerners ever take up arms and seize back the territory. So in effect, the Derry Cinderellas are left sucking thistles while their Belfast stepmothers keep all the jam for themselves and the two ugly sisters, Ballymena and Lisburn.

My job, so far as I can make out, is to make Belfast spread the jam a little more fairly. But from what my new staff tell me, and from what I've seen already this week, I'd have a better chance hitching a lift back home in Hillary's new jet. Or indeed convincing Maggie to move over here and join me . . . There's another one gone.

Be sure and apologize to Mom for me. Ah, well, you never know. Maybe your grandkids will be half-Irish. Wish me luck.

So long and slán (stay safe)
Your loving son
David

Schumann's Shoemakers
Dublin Road, Roslindale
Boston, MA

Dear David

I had no doubt at all you'd love Ireland – after all, didn't you grow up here in Boston, the biggest Irish city in the world?

And yes, they know how to pack away the drink. But watch yourself: a man can get fond of it. Next thing you know, he starts doing impersonations of his bosses – and winds up pitching his tent 3,000 miles away. Take my advice and stick to the Guinness. Whiskey is a drink for madmen. Just ask your Uncle Ernie, soon as we can get him dried out again.

I read Mom your letter. Thank God her eyes are gone, so I was able to skip lightly over your comments about me and Sally O'Cooley. For the love of Mike, I've spent a full quarter-century paying through the nose for that; could you ever let it go? She's actually forgotten all about it – God bless the Alzheimer's. But we'll see how smart your mouth is after fifty years of your own marriage. If you ever get there, that is. Chrissake, even if you got off the mark this year, you'd be eighty-seven by then – fifteen years older than I am now.

Your problem, Dave – and it's a family failing, believe me – is that you're just too damn happy. Always were. I blame myself. We should have beaten you more. Even as a child, nothing bothered you. Back when you started Forest Green Grade School and that big, fat bully spat in your lunch box, you didn't complain.

You simply took it as part of the natural progression of things and, as soon as she wasn't looking, urinated into her juice flask. You took a terrible pounding for that, but you came home smiling. Three missing teeth, I remember, but still smiling.

And you remember back when you were playing hoops for Boston U? And that center from the Fighting Irish ribbed you with his elbow nine times in the first quarter? Nine times he hit you and you didn't even flinch. He knew if he got you ejected, they'd walk the game – even if you were only a lousy six-two. But you never took him on and just kept shooting hoop after hoop. The guy would have got clean away with it, too, if Mom hadn't impaled him with her umbrella during the time-out. I think he wound up singing alto in the Notre Dame choir.

Your mother reckons that nothing ever bothers me, either. She's probably right. And your granddad, Old Poppy, was as laid back as they come. Never lost a night's sleep over anything, whether it was running hooch with Joey K in the '20s or trying to feed a family of eight in the '30s. Me, I had only you to worry about – and sure, you were no problem at all. God may have only granted us one child, but He damn sure gave us a good one.

The difficulty with being so happy, however, is that women are drawn to you. Like flies to a bookie's corpse. They just can't resist men who are relaxed – and who they can relax around, be natural around. It sure beats having to put on a palette of make-up before you get up for breakfast.

You're not bad looking, either, granted. 'Course, you were genetically protected by your mother. You can thank her for your dimples, the chocolate eyes – and for missing out on my chin. You're the first Schumann in 100 years who hasn't worn a beard. (Though, in fairness to your Aunt Ida, she did try the electrolysis.) And it's better than even money that you'll die with a head of raven-black hair.

But good looks and charm aren't enough to make a marriage. And much as your mother and I loved Maggie, it was never going to work with you pair. You were two of a laid-back kind. You really need someone who can slap you around a little, and I don't mean in a playful way. Someone with a bit of fire who can get under your skin, who needles you, motivates you, irritates you . . . scares you even. Someone who makes you want to try harder so that you deserve them. Someone who challenges you. But don't fret (not that you would anyway), I found mine, Old Poppy got his, and sure as God made bad-tempered women, you'll get yours, too. Oh, and your mother has long forgiven you for Maggie. She didn't fancy redheaded grandkids anyway.

I think you should consider cultivating a more somber face. Not only would it filter out a few of the light-headed young things who buzz around you, but a bit of gravitas might suit your new political career. It was all right when you were a newspaperman – they're supposed to make fun of people – but in politics, you could easily wind up a lightweight or a glad-hander. Especially now in these recessionary times. No-one trusts a smiler. We like them, sure. Everybody loves a comedian – but you'd never leave him in charge of the money.

Just look at The Boss. Since the day and hour he was elected, he's barely cracked a smile. Five thousand people losing their jobs every day – the last thing he wants is a picture of himself whooping it up on the front of the *New*

York Times. You did very well to spot him out of the gate, by the way. I was sure it'd be Hill. Hoped it for a long time, too. But day one, you recognized him as a guy who uses his own brain, not anybody else's. And it's a damn fine brain at that. So far.

And I know Derry isn't the dream posting, like Paris or Rome, but it's your first game in the big league. So learn from it, enjoy it and you'll be back with us before you know it. Never forget, you're very lucky you weren't straight out the door like some people wanted you. Bad enough the damn cigar, but you had to go and sprinkle yogurt on the dress . . .

I'm enclosing, as you asked, a DVD of the last couple of episodes of *Scrubs*. Can't believe they won't let you download them online. But you're right to assume that somebody's watching everything you're doing on your computer. And it wouldn't do for the US's first International Envoy to Londonderry to get caught breaking 500 copyright laws no-one's ever heard of just to get his fix of a fully dressed Sarah Chalke. There's a gizmo you can now buy that allows you to beam your favorite TV channels from home into any computer in the world. Totally legally. So I'll get your cousin Sam to check it out – soon as we can get him dried out again.

In the meantime, keep your head down and work hard (ha, ha).

All our love
Pop and Mom

PS The one thing I remember Old Poppy telling me about Derry is that it was home to some of the best smugglers in the world. He and Joey K did some business with a rogue called McGinlay, who somehow managed to keep our boys in half-decent bourbon when they were billeted on the Foyle in the '40s. I think his son is called Tommy and last heard of (twenty-five years ago) was training to be a lawyer in the town. Thieving is clearly still in the blood. Look him up if you get a chance. Or, on second thoughts, given your new job, run a mile when you hear his name mentioned.

Whitman House, Derry

Dear Pop

Thanks for the letter and the *Scrubs* DVD – which, typically, was confiscated by the boys at the front gate, watched in its entirety, then destroyed as a 'pirate copy'.

In fairness to them, though, they did tell me that they were two particularly good episodes, and that I'll really enjoy them when they're aired here in a year's time. (No prizes for guessing which president our security team voted for last time out.) In future, fire stuff into the consulate in Boston, and get them to stick it into the next diplomatic pouch heading this way.

For years, the Irish have been using their pouches from Dublin to smuggle out Tayto cheese and onion crisps, which, apparently, are the crack cocaine of potato chips but aren't yet distributed in the States. They've also been known to send over the odd bottle of *poitín*, sometimes known as 'the cratur', a 140-proof brand of homemade whiskey, which is illegal across the globe apart from in two North Korean nuclear facilities. (At least we'll have no bother with Uncle Ernie's Christmas present this year.)

Talking of which, I had no bother tracking down your lawyer pal McGinlay – he's a major player over here now. He took me on a walking tour of the city during which he confessed that the 'bourbon' his old man was feeding our GI Joes in WWII was actually *poitín* colored with cold tea. He also reckons that's why so many of our guys married Derry women.

McGinlay, who's better known as Tommy 'Bowtie', is a little shy of fifty, I'd reckon. Though it's hard to be sure, as he's not averse to a drop of the cratur himself. Big, jowlish face, bulbous nose, and sharp, beady eyes that miss nothing – all capped off with this untamable wiry red hair, "thicker than a whin bush", he assures me. Dresses in the dark, too, by the looks of things, but at least the stains on his jacket and pants match.

Fascinating man, though. Remembered Old Poppy very well – not from the war, naturally, but from his two visits to Ireland in the '70s. And thank you, sincerely, for never telling me what he and Tommy's old man were up to – and for not writing it down in your letter. I'd have been on the next plane out of here to downtown Tehran.

McGinlay, besides running his very successful criminal practice (ie he defends criminals), is also an electoral agent for two Westminster MPs and a couple of Irish senators. When I told the Dublin office I was meeting him, they were delighted. It's like getting a sit-down with Don Corleone on his daughter's wedding day – only Tommy Bowtie is better connected. (And knows where just as many bodies are buried, too, if what my cleaner Jeannie, a Derry native, tells me is true.)

Anyhow, Tommy collected me at my office yesterday morning and we walked up the river to the city center. He prefers talking outdoors and on the move – and he asked me to leave my iPhone behind me. Not so we wouldn't get interrupted, but because "they are both tracking devices and recording devices". With anybody else, you'd suspect paranoia, but Tommy holds the Irish record for having the most clients murdered over the past twenty-five years, so I dropped the cell into my desk drawer.

The riverfront walk is something else. Our compound is right on the water, built on the bones of an old army base a couple of miles from the city center. I'd only ever come in and out by car and didn't even know there was a back gate until Tommy led me out it and up the riverbank path. The view would stop you in your tracks. It's hard to believe you're in a city, there's so much green. Some of the woods here are maybe 3,000 years old.

Across the river from the gate is a huge forest park, which rises gently away from you, allowing you to spot some beautiful old buildings peeping out of the trees. The entire way into the town I spent staring up at the opposite bank, pointing out landmarks that Tommy identified for me. Couple of magnificent bridges, too: the new one, which is the longest suspension bridge in Ireland, and the old one, the only double-decker bridge on the island.

And then you have the center. Pop, you have to come and see the Old City. We only *think* Boston is historic. They have a complete set of seventeenth-century walls, forty feet high in places, with original battlements wide enough to drive a truck around. A complete set, I repeat; unmatched in Western Europe, or so they tell me. A full mile and a bit around, too, with views you wouldn't get from the top of the Prudential Tower. According to Tommy Bowtie, the eighteenth-century Protestant bishop of Derry, a wonderful old character called Hervey, used to interview potential curates by inviting them up to his palace on the city's walls, feeding them full of sherry, then making them strip naked and run around the ramparts. Whoever won the race got the job.

I won't even start trying to fill you in on the buildings you can see from the walls. Derry is Ireland's oldest Christian settlement, so you've stuff dating back 1,400 years, maybe more. (And here on the left, we have Dick Cheney's first cave drawing . . .)

Even more entertaining than Tommy Bowtie's tour, however, was his potted guide to the town and its politics. I think I learned more in those two hours than if I'd read every CIA briefing note or Irish history book ever published. But like virtually everyone I've met here, he's totally focused on the future – there's no reheating old ashes. The war is over, even if the British still like to pretend it was nothing but a criminal insurgency against their honest rule.

Occasionally, there are flare-ups, like when some people dare argue that all the victims of the conflict should have parity. And again, this harks back to who mistreated whom more. But, as Tommy wisely said, if people are busy making money, they're not going to have time to worry about it. Time and cash cure all wounds.

The payback for Tommy's tour (and the excellent 'fish supper' he treated me to in Fiorentini's Café) is that I have to do an interview on Radio Mountrose next week with his niece, Ellie. Mountrose is a tiny little border town, unremarkable other than that one in four of its five thousand populace are employed by an American pharmaceutical company, Dunsuffrin (they make headache powders). But the radio station's quite popular and widely listened to in Derry, and it'd be a coup for her to get me before the BBC, so I signed up for what's called a soft-focus 'puff piece'. That is, no hard questions: what do you love most about Ireland etc? It'll be a breeze, Tommy promised me. So why do I suddenly feel I'm sitting in the Last Chance Saloon with a pair of deuces, while Wild Bill Hickok's just filled his straight?

Anyhow, I'll report back afterwards. In the meantime, do what you can with the *Scrubs* DVD. If all else fails, you can rig up the webcam to the TV and I'll start getting up at three in the morning to watch it live.

Big hello to Mom. Tell her I'll ring her on Saturday when I get back from Temple (ahem).

So long and slán
Your loving son
David

Whitman House, Derry

Dear Mayor Boyce

I would be delighted to take you up on your suggestion to visit you in Mountrose just as soon as our respective staff can organize a date.

As you may have heard, I'm doing a (telephone) interview with your local radio station the day after tomorrow, which will give me a chance to acquaint myself with some of the issues affecting your town.

I'll call when I'm done with it, and we'll set something up soonest.

Yours respectfully
David Schumann

Town Hall, Mountrose

<u>URGENT</u>

Dear Mr Schumann

I wasn't aware you were going on Mountrose Radio. Please tell me it's not with Ellie McGinlay? Contact me as soon as you get this.

Yours sincerely
Mayor Montgomery Boyce

PS Seriously, you have no idea what you're getting into.

Whitman House, Derry

Dear Montgomery

The next time, would you please pick up a goddamned phone? Soft focus, my ass. She carved me open like a Thanksgiving ham. Then the BBC picked it up and ran the whole damn thing as, of course, did the anarchists on YouTube.

I'll meet you next Monday – here – and you can advise me how I'll ever be able to go out in public again.

Yours
David

McGinlay Solicitors
Liars' Row, Dunavady

Dear Dave

Sincere apologies for the niece's lynching of you. All I can say in her defence is her last boyfriend was an American – and she cut him off at the short hair as well.

The dirty little secret I couldn't let you in on is that you can never say you've arrived in Derry until Ellie knocks the tar out of you on air. It's a rite of passage. But happily, you're now one of us.

I was one of her first victims myself when I agreed to do what I thought was an Ask-Your-Friendly-Lawyer slot. You should console yourself by knowing that what *you* got, *I* got in shovelfuls. And not only am I her uncle – but I'm also a major shareholder in the bloody radio station.

I'll call by on Friday night, if you're up for it, and take you out for a bite, by way of atonement. There's a wonderful seafood restaurant, the Drunken Duck, over the border in Stroove, and on the way home, we can drive by Ellie's house and throw rocks through her windows.

Just a word on my address, as above, by the way. It used to be known as Drumbridge Avenue. But then, two local politicians went and opened constituency offices just down from me, so the locals jokingly re-named the street. Then some smart-arse made a formal proposal at Council, and here we are. At least you'll have no trouble finding us.

Slán go fóill
Tommy

Whitman House, Derry

Dear Pop

You'll probably have heard the interview on the net by now so can understand why I won't be doing any others for a while. I also sent all the staff in Derry and across the island a why-the-hell-didn't-you-warn-me memo. Only to discover that each and every one of them were in on the joke. Rite of passage? More like bend over and insert right up your passage.

The Boss's people got in touch to let me know no lasting harm had been done. They were actually very sympathetic and wired me across an interview that Bush Junior did with Irish TV reporter Carole Coleman. It made me feel so much better. Coleman, who's a tiny inoffensive-looking thing, kicked the leader of the free world around the White House office then mopped up the blood with Dubya's $500 tie.

I didn't mind so much Ellie's questions about Iraq, Iran and Afghanistan – we're all pretty well drilled in the new script – but she was a bit sharp, even a bit personal, about the whole Palestinian question. Then again, I'm around long enough to handle that. And besides, I've written two Op-Ed pieces calling for an end to the blockades of Gaza, so she can stick that in her trendy left-wing peace pipe and smoke it.

But she caught me flatfooted by asking me when exactly the CIA had ceased the practice of taking guys through Ireland they were about to torture. A classic when-did-you-stop-beating-your-wife question. And, of course, we were guilty as Nixon. I tried to point out that The Boss had stopped all that now, and that all past abuses would be investigated. So, quick as a flash, she wanted to know how much compensation we'd be paying for these breaches of international law. And my "Um, I'll check back," so I've been told, is probably going to cost us a new computer component factory in County Limerick.

But even that didn't blindside me as much as the Dunsuffrin stuff. Jeez, the plant employs 1,200 people in Mountrose; why in the hell does she seem so intent on shutting it down? Of course they test their product on animals! My God, they'd be crazy not to: it's a narcotic. But Ellie, who naturally is a lifelong tree-hugger, quoted three different newspaper reports in which the site manager, Chris Diaz, promised there'd be no testing in Ireland. And naturally, there was. And the *Derry Standard* got a whole roll of pictures of innocent rats being murdered . . . sorry, tested. And now the country's up in arms.

It's a PR disaster, so I've lined up a meeting with Diaz for next Thursday during which I'm going to kick his ass and shut down the vivisection unit, or 'death chamber', as Ellie referred to it.

I'm not saying that the natives haven't got a point. International business allows little room for morality. It has always been cheaper, and less politically sensitive for us, to keep dirty industries, torture and animal testing at arm's length – or at least at a couple of degrees of deniability. Which means we often export them. We also pay lower wages overseas and expect towns like Mountrose to kiss our well-fed asses anytime we drop in for a coffee. Because, of course, if they don't, we'll find some other Hicksville that'll be only too glad of our 'friendship'.

The trouble with that approach (apart from our responsibilities to the planet and mankind) is that too many people have become wise to us. And we're running out of back alleys to crap all over.

The best part of the interview, you'll have to agree, was the final question. Came right out of left-field. I was curled up in the fetal position on my office couch, staring at the speakerphone and wondering where she was going to hit me next, when all of a sudden,

she said, "And finally, Mr Envoy, what's your favorite thing about Ireland?"

Without thinking, I replied, "The people: they're so welcoming." And in fairness, she then laughed as hard as I did.

I finally got to meet my nemesis face to face over the weekend, and she was every bit as warm to me in person. By sheer coincidence, Tommy swears, Ellie was in the same restaurant he and I were in on Friday night. And *Derry Standard* editor Mary Slavin was treating her to a celebratory you-kicked-the-shit-out-of-the-Yank dinner.

Gotta say, Ellie inherited few of Tommy's genes, other than maybe his clever-bastard lawyering skills. She looks far less shrewish and much younger than I expected – kinda like a twenty-something Nicole Kidman, only less severe. Great smile, and you can see the humor in her eyes – all of which, of course, didn't come across in the phone interview. She does have the dreaded McGinlay red hair, though hers is more of a dark copper color, and as straight as Tommy's is wiry.

Anyhow, after a couple of fairly cool introductions, I sent her over a bottle of wine to pretend there were no hard feelings. But apparently there were on her side, and she sent it straight back. Then, as they were leaving, I nodded over goodnight, and she looked right through me, before chiming out, "See you, Uncle Tommy. Thanks for lining me up another patsy." Thus emptying the two of us with the same one-liner. Tommy burst out laughing and assured me she really liked me. If she hadn't, she'd have returned the bottle in her trademark, less-than-traditional manner.

As I watched her leave the car park, she looked out of her little eco-car and gave me that exact same shit-eating grin the Fordham center gave me when he pulled down my shorts at the end of Boston U's worst mauling in living memory. And, I have to confess, I felt something stir in me. Maybe it's because I'm not used to being beaten. Or maybe, just maybe, if I'm to be honest, it's because she's the type I might have gone for once – back before she made me a eunuch . . .

Oh, God, don't tell me this is how it's going to be for me.

Thanks for the *Scrubs* live relay, by the way, but I think I'm going to get it all sorted out this week. One of Tommy's sisters lives in America and has been sending a TV feed back home to Ireland for a couple of years. So I'm going to watch it at his house from now on.

You know – if it wasn't for the TV and the cranky women, I'd almost think of staying here.

So long and slán
Your loving son
David

PS Big hello to Mom – and don't tell her the bit about the red hair.

Town Hall, Mountrose

Dear Dave

Thanks for the chat yesterday, and for not taking our radio station personally. As I explained, I did try to phone you four times. It's just that your people are far too good at protecting you. And it seems telling them you're mayor of Mountrose ranks right up there with being the man who comes to unclog the toilet.

By way of explanation for Ellie McGinlay, all I can say is that when I was a youngster here and got a new pair of school shoes, the rest of the class would launch a sneak attack at break time to scuff all the shine off the leather. To teach me the meaning of modesty. And, I'm afraid, Ellie is a graduate of the same school.

Console yourself, at least, that she didn't ask if you'd ever presided over one of the IRA's internal courts, like she did with her Uncle Tommy. Absolutely no truth in it whatsoever. But Tommy, as you may or may not know, suffers from an irritable bowel, and Ellie had a side-bet with her producer that she could activate it. (She did.)

Most of the time, though, she's right on the money with her facts. When the jockey 'King Size' Barkley tried to deny he'd ever been involved in race fixing, she pulled out a sworn affidavit, signed by eight different bookies, outlining why they would never do business with him. King Size, incidentally, also developed an irritable bowel that very day.

And yes, everyone knows by now that the pictures she produced of me on the tourism conference in Amsterdam weren't Photoshopped, as I tried to insist at the time. House of Pleasure my backside. It cost me a new Alfa Romeo for the wife. And by the by, for future reference, the girls inside looked nothing like the lady with the rubber attachments on the poster out front.

So please put the whole McGinlay experience behind you and assure yourself that we still very much value your friendship and your interest in our region. Your great nation makes a massive contribution, not only to our town, but to the island as a whole. You fund about one in five jobs in the South and about one in eight in the North. Just look at Derry: between DuPont and Seagate, your companies have fed and clothed three entire generations there.

Anyhow, just a couple of further points to be aware of before you meet Dr Chris Diaz. First, she (note, not he) is extremely plausible. Listens to all your arguments, nods sympathetically, promises you she'll do all she can and immediately forgets you the minute you're out the door. It's not even that she's smooth – she's too sincere to appear smooth – rather, she disarms you with gentleness. But for all that, she made me understand very early that she runs Mountrose – not me. And I imagine that you're going to hit a similar bump.

'Course, she's helped no end by the fact that she's got a face and body that . . . Well, put it like this, if you saw her appearing in a late-night movie, you'd be drawing the curtains and bolting the door. Long, slim legs, spectacular black curly hair, and this generous Latina mouth with whiter teeth than a Mormon god. Add in half a yard of cleavage that would put a shake in your hand, and two perfect hazel eyes, and you'd wonder how in the hell anyone gets any work done at that plant at all. I'm sure glad I'm not employed there; I'd need a saline drip. (And yes, I have a very obvious weakness, Dave. But at least I'm up front about it.) No boyfriend as yet, and she's far too straight to mess around with married men . . . sadly. But a man can still fantasise. And regularly does.

You'll probably win the vivisection argument with her, but only because she hates the testing herself. Not that she's a bunny lover – rather, it eats into her profit margins. And it would suit her no end to tell her bosses back home that the envoy is leaning on her. They've another plant in Indonesia that's more equipped for that sort of thing (ie a less politicised workforce and a tamer media), so you could have it phased out within months.

Truth be told, other than Ellie, most of the locals aren't too worried about the rat farm at all. Country people tend to have a much more pragmatic attitude to animals than big-city folk like Ms McGinlay, categorising them into three basic types: food, pests and exotic. And rats definitely come into the second class.

What more of us in Mountrose are concerned about, however, is the persistent rumour – suggestion even – that a number of Dunsuffrin workers are deploying their drug-manufacturing skills in private practice.

We've had three serious incidents involving Ecstasy in the town in the last three months, including one death. And from what the police in Derry tell us, there's been a real upsurge in E use in the city there as well, and the batches seem to be coming from our little town. Whether they're being made inside or outside the plant still isn't clear. But, confidentially, the police have asked for access to the factory to spy on a group of night-shift workers who are known bad lads. Thus far, however, Dr Diaz is insisting there is no evidence other than gossip; and she isn't budging.

So, we'd all be grateful if you could do what you could. You've a reputation for being quite charming yourself, and I'll concede that you're not altogether terrifying looking. Is this, perhaps, where we get to see what happens when two irresistible objects collide?

Look forward to hooking up with you on Saturday night to compare notes. Tell Tommy it's his turn to bring the beer. I'll bring the cards (long-standing joke; I always refuse to play with Tommy's packs).

Yours
Monty

Schumann's Shoemakers, Boston

Dear David

Thanks for buzzing us up for the webchat last night. Your mother is always particularly relieved to see you in the flesh, even if her glaucoma means you look even fuzzier round the edges to her than you do to me. Also means, of course, she can't spot the bags under your eyes, you naughty boy, you.

I tend to agree with you, though: letters are a much more private option. And there's a certain sanctity that goes with sealing an envelope. Theoretically, at least, a letter's contents are protected under federal law and can't come back to bite you on the ass in court – not like email or live-cam. Rest assured, ever since we got the computers in the shop, I've abided by your advice and have never entered anything into a machine that I wouldn't want to read on the front page of the *New York Times*. (I actually have that very dictum printed out above your Uncle Ernie's machine – though I've added that you should never try to look at any pictures you wouldn't see on the front of the *NYT*, either. God bless his perverted old heart.)

Exciting times for you over on th'oul sod (as my pal McKenna would call it). Not sure what angle Tommy is working, either, though from what you tell me, he seems about as straight as you're ever going to get for a lawyer. And I like the fact he has a reputation for spotting young talent and mentoring it all the way to the top. It'll do you good to have someone smarter than you giving you advice for once.

You didn't mention if you'd met the niece since? Or maybe you're saving your breath mints for Dr Diaz? Mom would definitely prefer the Texan option; she's getting tired of your penchant for redheads. Me, I don't think we'll ever cure you of it. Talking of which, Maggie came into the shop this morning to get a pair of heels done. She's got herself a job down in Washington in the PR department. She's going to give it the full four years, which means she'll be thirty-eight by the time she's done. And just in case you're wondering, no, we cannot wait that long.

By the way, I love the fact that you're playing private detective with the druggies. I'll bet your mother's teeth they're making the stuff in the factory. Joey K and your granddaddy pulled the same stunt way back in the 1920s. They bought a cola-bottling operation up in Worcester, though, naturally, three out of every four bottles they produced was full of 5% beer. Never got caught, either, so long as they kept the front-of-house clean and paid the local cops their cut. Funny thing was, they made a lot more money on the cola than they ever did on the beer. But I think they just wanted the rush.

The difference with your guys is that their stuff is illegal. And it has been known to kill people . . .

Let me know how you get on at the cards. Don't sell off the farm.

All our love
Pop and Mom

                                            Whitman House, Derry

<u>PRIVATE</u>

Dear Monty

What can I say? She charmed me, just like you said she would. If I'd been any more of a puppy dog, I'd have rolled over on my back to let her tickle my belly. (Or possibly even climbed up on her leg.)

It didn't help that she was en route to a cocktail party and was wearing this very short, very low-cut yellow dress. Honest to God, I nearly snapped my neck trying to keep my eyes on her face.

"Excuse the frock," she grinned at me. "I've been

summoned to some county councillor's goddamn retirement. Corporate HQ insist I spend at least three hours a week pimping myself out... I mean networking. Jackasses. And because I'm on duty, I can't even take a damn drink."

Yep, totally disarming. And Jeez, what a smile. Would get a rise from a gelding. Lot younger than I thought, too; CEO at twenty-nine. I was thirty-one before I made editor and, as you recall, I consider myself one of the smartest people I know.

I led off with the vivisection unit and got a result straightaway. No problem, she said, and flashed me another smile; it's already earmarked for closure. And here's the kicker: she's going to let *me* make the announcement next week as a mark of good faith. And yes, we Yanks must stick together.

In return, however, she asked me to give her two weeks to complete her own investigation into the bad lads at her plant.

Cute move. But I was ready. Tommy Bowtie had given me a few names – Dennis O'Neary, aka Nero, Fergal McDowd and John Hawkson – three guys who work in the plant and have been selling tablets around the local clubs. So I shook my head and told her to drum these men out of the plant straightaway. We couldn't take the chance of them producing more stuff.

She looked at me for a second, smiled again, then wrinkled her nose into a disarmingly soft 'no' – like I was giving her an option on this and not a direct order. I only think I'm a diplomat.

"Listen," she said, "you're right about Nero. He's a nightmare, and we're doing all we can to run him out the back door. But his drug sideline is absolutely unconnected to Dunsuffrin. The problem is that if you put it on the record, we'll have to launch a full inquiry, which, let's face it, is a totally pointless exercise, given that you couldn't smuggle mouseshit out of this place, much less manufacture it."

I gave her an unconvinced look, so she put her elbows onto her desk and let her head sink wearily into her hands.

"The only chemical compounds allowed on this site are the powders we mix together for Dunsuffrin. Anything else – even nasal spray or asthma inhalers – is banned. Instant dismissal. We can't take the chance. You wouldn't believe the controls: security checks coming in, security checks going out; we're not even allowed to employ anyone who has a link to anyone with a drug problem. If we find you have a relative or close friend with a narcotics habit, you're out the door. No argument, and no comeback, either – it's federal law. You yourself, Mr Schumann, could never get a job in here now, because of your cousin Sam."

Clearly, she'd done her homework, so I nodded to concede the point. Albeit nervously.

"So you've had your suspicions about Nero and his colleagues for some time?" I pressed her.

"Of course we did, but we'd no evidence."

"Well, now you've a formal allegation. From a government envoy, no less." (I can play the important card when I have to.)

She shook her head. "It's not enough. If you're serious about getting these guys, why not find who's running them? They're not bright enough to try something like this themselves. Christ, Dave, I could even help you. We could stick up a couple of hidden cameras and mikes to monitor the night shift. See who they're talking about. Shit knows, it wouldn't be the first time. You put it on the record, though, and you're tying my hands."

What she was saying did make a lot of sense. And she had given me the vivisection victory for the press. So I sighed an okay and was rewarded with yet another one of those smiles. And yes, it was worth it.

But the best part, Monty, and I hope you're sitting down when you read this, happened as we were winding up the meeting.

"Now, if you'll excuse me," she said, "I have to get moving or I'll be stuck at the damn clergy's table like I was the last time. Sheila, my PA, will show you out. Oh, and I'm free next Thursday night, by the way."

"Excuse me?" I replied, confused.

"Next Thursday night, say eight o'clock at La Trattoria in Derry. Me and you. Eat. Chat. Maybe even take a little walk afterwards? Sheila has been telling me for the past hour how you're back in play after your girl back home dumped you for the bright lights of DC. Truth is, I was going to let Sheila have you for herself, but then I got a look at you . . ."

I opened my mouth to try to speak but could get nothing out.

"Chrissake, Dave," she smiled at me. "If I waited for you to ask, we'd still be dancing round this desk at Christmas. Don't worry, I'll not bite. Well, not unless you want me to . . . What do you say?"

I took a deep breath. "I'd say that sounds like fun."

"Oh, it will be," she grinned. "I promise."

So, Monty boy, I'm afraid you're going to have to look elsewhere for your midlife crisis, as I'm taking this one. Can't wait to see Ellie McGinlay's face; she'll be convinced it's all a CIA plot.

See you on Saturday at the poker. I'll be the guy with the smile on his face.

All the best
Dave

                                  Police Headquarters
                                    Strand Road, Derry

Dear Mr Schumann

Further to our conversation yesterday, we've done a quick breakdown of our drugs seizures in the past six months, and the preliminary results are just as we feared. The number of tablets confiscated is up by 120% on the previous six months, and a little over 200% on the half-year before that. Also, the size, markings and contents of more than four-fifths of the seizures are virtually identical (they were made in the same place). So by our reckoning, both use and supply in the Derry area have at least doubled in the past year.

Unfortunately, however, at least one batch of the new influx has been adulterated with a cheap but very powerful amphetamine, which we believe was the primary factor in the three hospitalisations in Mountrose – and in the death of Peggy O'Whelan, who, according to the pathologist, had taken just four tablets.

We have no specific evidence – other than unreliable hearsay – that the drugs are coming from Mountrose, and I would have to concur with Dr Diaz that it is very improbable that they're emanating from the Dunsuffrin plant. The chemical make-up of the product suggests it's much more likely they're being made in a lab in Britain, possibly Glasgow, as the same type of tabs are in widespread circulation there. They're then smuggled over here by a local entrepreneur. A student, perhaps? Or even one of the many football fans from here who travel to Scotland to watch Rangers or Celtic games?

While I appreciate Dr Diaz's offer to monitor certain members of her staff, you should advise her to be very careful about breaching privacy laws. The police have powers to sanction such operations; you do not. Furthermore, I wish to remind you that should Dr Diaz unearth any impropriety, she is obliged to bring her findings to me immediately. I repeat – immediately.

(Off the record: you should also warn her that her surveillance techniques are unlikely to be of the standards required by our courts. So anything on them would need to be corroborated by other evidence – a police witness, or, better again, a police seizure.)

Your second concern was that gangsters masquerading as dissident paramilitaries might somehow be benefiting from the increase in illegal drug use here, whether it be by directly selling the drugs, controlling the chain, or simply 'taxing' the pushers. Again, we have no evidence of this, but I accept it's possible. Very possible.

I respectfully advise you, however, to allow the Police Service of Northern Ireland (PSNI) to pursue these avenues of investigation with the professionalism for which we are known – and without interference. We will keep you updated on all developments.

Yours sincerely
Chief Superintendent Edward O'Conway

Whitman House, Derry

Dear Pop

There's a saying over here about people who are very lucky: they could fall into the Foyle and come up with a salmon in their mouth. Well, that's how I felt yesterday when Chris – I mean Dr Diaz – summoned me to Mountrose for a private screening of some super-hot film. (Get your mind out of the gutter, old man. I'm talking about the surveillance tapes, of course.)

The cameras and mikes had been set up in the canteen just a week ago, above the seat where the three bad lads normally sit. And the night before last, they paid for themselves in spades.

Chris already had the TV in her office switched on and the film disc paused at the compromising spot by the time I got to her office. Chad Scarpa, the plant's big, bald, black chief of security, was sitting in an armchair beside the set, holding the remote. I was able to tell from the on-screen timer that the night-shift boys had come a cropper at exactly 2.08 that morning.

"Who else has seen this?" I asked Chad before he hit the play button.

"No-one," he replied, pointing to Chris. "Doctor

Diaz insisted this would be a one-man operation. A second mouth can't keep a secret and all that."

I nodded my approval, and we sat back on the Italian leather sofa she has for guests and watched.

The three boys were sitting in the corner of the deserted factory café, drinking Coke and eating Mars Bars. Yet another reason that people who work nights die ten years younger.

"What time's he due in at?" asked the tallest of the three, a long-haired, strong-jawed jock with muscular biker forearms.

"Nero," said Chad, talking over the playback.

"Leaving Derry at four," replied a fat, red-faced almost-dwarf.

"John Hawkson," voiced-over Chad.

"Due to arrive at the factory for his collection at quarter to five at the latest," continued Hawkson. "He's got one stop on the way down."

"Who's meeting him?" asked Nero, glancing sideways at the café counter twenty yards away.

"I am," said the third of the group, a tall, copper-haired, slightly younger youth.

"Fergal McDowd," whispered Chad.

"What's the plan?" pressed Nero.

"'Sactly as before," said Hawkson. "Billy pulls into the lay-by just outside the town to consult his charts . . ."

"Billy Cotton's a van driver from Derry," explained Chad quickly. "We service all the chemists there at cost, as a goodwill gesture. He collects here once a month and delivers to them all."

". . . Fergal pulls up on his bike alongside to offer him directions," Hawkson went on, "takes the package from Billy, pays the docket, and Billy drives on up to the factory for his consignment of Dunsuffrin tablets."

On screen, Nero looked from one of them to another. "Okay, but next time, change it round a bit," he said menacingly. "We gotta be very careful. These youngsters are whacking way too much of the stuff into themselves. Bringing far too much attention on the town."

"It said on the news that the tabs Peggy O'Whelan took were contaminated," argued O'Dowd.

"Bullshit!" retorted Nero. "That silly little bitch took eight of them; of course they're going to say they're contaminated. They're trying to shut us down. Look, according to our man in Derry, this stuff is coming direct from Holland. Every batch is quality-checked out in that big testing center at the Anything Goes rave complex before they send it. If they were any safer, we'd be making them here."

All three men laughed.

But O'Dowd still wasn't convinced. "Who sold her the stuff? The O'Whelan girl?" he pressed again.

"John-Joe McGownie," cut in Hawkson. "He told my brother, Mick. He figured he'd have a better chance with her if she was buzzing a little."

"Each man kills the thing he loves," sighed Nero. He raised his eyes knowingly, then smiled tolerantly. "We've all been there. John-Joe's not a bad lad. Tell him if I ever catch him selling more than five at a time, I'll bust his hole for him."

"No action, so?"

Nero shrugged uncomfortably. "He offloaded two hundred tabs for us on New Year's weekend. All his school buddies. And besides, he's a pal of our Conal's . . ."

As Nero was speaking, a café worker came over to the table to remove the rubbish. Nero checked his watch and stood up to go, his two friends following quickly.

The picture went black, and Chad stood up and turned off the TV.

I was stunned, not only by the trio's scant regard for human life – but also by the fact we'd caught them cold.

Chad grinned over at me. "Great picture, too – just like HDTV. So, we hand this into the cops?"

Chris nodded instinctively. "Give it to O'Conway," she agreed.

I was still mindful, however, about the lecture O'Conway had given me about playing amateur detective, so I wasn't so sure. "It might be more useful just to tell him what we know from it," I said. "Tell him we got information from a cast-iron source who has to remain anonymous. That lets us hang on to the camera as a resource. Ultimately, we want to find out where this stuff is coming from, but if we fire all our ammo now, we're only going to mow down the front line."

Chris bit her lip for a second and then nodded. "You're dead right," she said. "Give O'Conway the details. Let him make the seizure and claim the glory, while we keep watching to see what else we can get."

Chad stuck up a warning finger. "You sure you don't want to cut the cops in? We could probably trust O'Conway not to blow the whistle on the camera until the whole thing is closed down."

"He wouldn't allow it," I insisted. "He couldn't help himself. He's too damn straight. That disc, I'd be pretty sure, is violating a couple of privacy laws – and probably breaching those lowlifes' human rights. And there's no way O'Conway could launch a search based on an illegal wire. Better he can tell his superiors he's getting his intelligence from a credible, though anonymous, source; someone who's using me as a conduit."

"So, what about Nero and the two boys?" Chris asked. "Do we have to keep them on payroll?"

"Just for the time being . . . to see where they lead us," I said to her. "For the meantime, let the police hang it all on Billy Cotton. It's possible Nero might believe it was just random luck."

"I wonder who 'our man in Derry' is?" remarked Chris.

"No idea," I replied, "but maybe Mr Cotton will tell us when he finds himself looking at a ten stretch for supplying."

As soon as I got home, I rang O'Conway and filled him in on as much as I could. He knows fine well there's a camera, but as long as I don't mention it and he doesn't ask, his ass is covered. He's simply acting on a high-grade tip-off.

Needless to say, he repeated his lecture about letting the professionals do their own jobs – but he did accept that they'd be hosting a surprise party for Mr Cotton tomorrow night. He also disclosed that Mr Cotton has dealings with some very hard boys in Dunavady – guys who weren't quite ready to give up their fight for Irish freedom and had retained some of their hardware. So it'll be interesting to see where his scoop takes us.

I'll give you a webshout on Saturday night after the poker to fill you in on what's happening. Oh, and settle yourself; the most you're allowed to lose at the table is ten pounds, so your shop is safe. Not that I'm ever going to get rich playing with these guys, though. Beats me why we don't just hand our money over to Monty Boyce at the start of the night and get drunk in peace.

Be sure and tell Mom that things are going very well with Chris – I seem to have broken the redheaded streak once and for all. I really like this one: she's modest, kind, and has a smile that just makes your day. And as you see from the pix I've wired you, absolutely gorgeous. Smart as a circus dog, too. First time I've ever felt I'm playing out of my league. Tommy Bowtie tells me that Ellie went ballistic when she heard and is convinced it's all part of Dunsuffrin's grand plan to cover up a litany of shady dealings. God bless her little commie heart.

Anyhow, I'll go now and post this before I head off to Tommy's for some live *Scrubs*. It's two in the morning here, but Tommy, like the devil, never sleeps.

So long and slán
Your loving son
David

Police Headquarters, Derry

PRIVATE AND CONFIDENTIAL

Dear Mr Schumann

Further to our conversation last week, here's the update on the drugs seizure on Friday evening.

For operational reasons, we decided to make the arrest just as Cotton's van was leaving the car park outside the Derry pharmacy he works for. (We decided not to hit him in Mountrose, as it might have suggested where the info came from.)

The van's storage compartment was full of licit drugs and medicines, so it looked momentarily as though we were going to have a long night ahead of us. You've got to hand it to these guys: if you're going to hide straw, stick it in a haystack. But Cotton realised right away he'd been tumbled and pointed to an unmarked white carton, about the size of a shoebox, sitting under a consignment of Viagra. So we opened that, and sure enough, the 2,000 tablets inside were all adorned with the tell-tale St Andrew's Cross marking. They've a street value of about £10,000, though we told the media it's twice that. We're still getting the tabs tested, but we're pretty sure they're the real deal (certainly would have been enough to light up all of Mountrose for the weekend).

Getting our man to talk, however, was a different proposition entirely. He either genuinely knows nothing or he's too scared to talk. Anyway, he was smart enough to get himself a lawyer before he talked to us – Kitty O'Carty, a very sharp operator, who refused to let him answer anything but name, rank and serial number. Kitty realises that while a 'no comment' interview can sit badly when it's read out before a jury in court, it generally plays a million times better than: "I dunnit, guv, but I'm really sorry." And, as I'm sure you're aware, ninety-nine out of a 100 people in this country are convicted out of their own mouths.

Cotton's entire defence, I'd imagine, will be that a man he didn't know put a gun to his head and made him carry the parcel. And I'll tell you, I've seen them win. But we'll be doing a thorough check on his old colleagues in Dunavady over the next couple of weeks, regardless. I also hope you will continue to pursue your own . . . avenues – and particularly the source which yielded us this most valuable breakthrough. But I again stress that you should call us immediately if you learn anything which can help us.

Seriously, Mr Schumann, leave the Nancy Drew stuff to us.

Best wishes
Chief Superintendent Edward O'Conway

Handwritten cover note on attached compliments slip:

<u>OFF THE RECORD</u>

You'd be doing us a big favour, Dave, if you could land us Nero or one of his cohorts next; it'd be a big PR coup. He's the dark lord out there. Though I appreciate you're hoping to get to the end of the supply line and are worried (rightly) that our boys will feck it up. Still, be sure and remember to leave the rough stuff to us – keep your judo holds for Dr Diaz's leather couch. (Incidentally, I happen to know a Scenes-of-Crime officer who just this week is offering a great deal on blue happy pills . . .)

Nearly forgot, Tommy Bowtie says you need a fourth player for your poker school – someone to keep Monty Boyce honest. It's a tall order, but I'll do what I can.

See you next Saturday – and thanks.

Ed

Whitman House, Derry

HIGHLY CONFIDENTIAL

Dear Ed

I was worried a little that you might be too straight to play cards with us, but Tommy assured me that any man who'd been a cop for twenty years would hold a few aces up his sleeve. And in your case, it was literally. Even Monty Boyce was impressed at how well you were dealing them from the bottom of the deck. And yes, of course you're welcome back, although you'll understand why we're getting Chad Scarpa to install two security cameras over the table. By the end of the night, though, we were so busy watching you that, typically, Boyce snuck in and took home the last pot. Good luck to him – he'll need it to keep his new girlfriend in gym socks.

Your seizure last week seems to have thrown a scare into the bad lads at the factory, so I hear. They haven't met up once since Cotton was 'lifted', as you say here, and are all casting one another distrusting glances when they pass in the canteen. At least that's according to my gorgeous mole (who, coincidentally, also has a gorgeous mole in a place where you will never get to see it).

Tommy was explaining to me that it was a favorite police tactic during the Troubles here: plant the seeds of doubt and make everyone suspect the other guy is an informer. Keeps them honest. I'm glad to see that some of the old methods can be so successfully applied in these non-paramilitary times. But it's also good that you no longer have the power to whack people you suspect of doing you harm, even if you catch them in the act of committing blatant crimes – as you did up to about ten years ago. Otherwise, Monty Boyce would never have made it out of the room on Saturday night.

Seriously, though, Cotton's arrest was a brilliant result and has put manners on his buddies. Even Ellie McGinlay felt obliged to praise the police operation on her morning program yesterday. Though it was a bit mean of her to suggest that it was sheer blind luck rather than careful planning. She's really miffed that Tommy won't clue her in on what's going on. And yes, it is essential to keep Mr Bowtie in the loop at all times. For my money, Tommy is the one person who tends to understand the full picture. The rest of us are mere bit players.

Tommy tells me, by the way, that Ellie is taking bets that Chris will ditch me as soon as I greenlight her factory-expansion proposals. Told him that she's nothing but a "cold, manipulative Texican control freak". While remaining a gentleman, let me assure you that my new girlfriend is anything but cold – and is absolutely no more manipulative or controlling than any other woman I've ever dated. As a very wise man once said, somebody has to do the spanking, and somebody has to be the spankee.

Anyway, I've managed to get £200 on, via Tommy, that I'll survive at least another month. I'm sure you or Monty will be happy to take it from me at the poker table at a later date.

See you on Saturday.

Dave

PS Don't forget those cable ties you promised me.

Tommy Bowtie writes:

Ed O'Conway was a great addition for the table. A straight man who could provide a little balance to Monty's comedy act. Honest, too, for all my messing, without being unduly burdened with it. A grown-up type of policeman who understands that rules are fine, but good results matter more. He's a Southerner, too – so has a natural disrespect for all authority. Northern-born cops tend to bow to the badge.

Chris, though, was a distraction Dave could have done without. Too much into the game. Flirting, teasing – and ultimately controlling. Anyhow, I'm always a bit doubtful of people who reach the top so quickly – there's only three possible reasons: their daddy is very rich; they're abnormally talented (which tends to mean borderline crazy); or they've kissed so much ass they're not real people any more. And Chris was neither of the first two . . .

FEBRUARY
♥

Whitman House, Derry

Dear Pop

Whoever said that a week is a long time in politics was born, grew old and died before the era of the internet and twenty-four-hour news.

This time yesterday, my life was very simple and the biggest problem I had was whether to shave before going to Chris's last night or stick with the rugged Brad Pitt before-he-went-sissy-boy look. (More of which later.)

Then it happened. The world caved in – or at least in Derry it did. And tonight, I'm up to my neck in shit and the local sewage plant is looking to install an overflow pipe into my living room.

Let me explain. On a good day here, as I've told you, it is very bad news when Belfast gets a major jobs development or cash injection. Belfast, like all evil stepmothers, is greedy, selfish and gloating in victory. Derry, however, has got used to its triumphalism and largely ignores it.

When Belfast swoops in and blatantly steals 700 jobs earmarked for Derry, however – well, that's a different matter entirely. It is tantamount to declaring war.

Worst of all options, though, is when Belfast nips in and steals 700 *American* jobs earmarked for Derry, and you're the guy whose sole purpose in life is to stop Belfast doing it.

I might as well have sold off the last lifeboat on the *Titanic*. There was no hiding place; all of a sudden, Derry was in uproar, and I was the enemy.

Tommy Bowtie tells me he's surprised I lasted a full month before they turned on me, although even he was shocked at the vitriol of the *Derry Standard* front-page headline: 'Yankee Poodle Pansy'. (Synopsis: I'm a lackey in the pay of Belfast, and Chris has told her gal-pals that certain parts of our relationship aren't, ah, firm enough. See pages two to ten for details.)

That was only the warm up. The ink on the *Standard* wasn't dry when BBC Radio Foyle door-stepped me at a breakfast meeting in the City Hotel and fried me up crispier than the bacon I was missing inside. ("Tell me, Mr Envoy, how in all conscience can you take a six-figure salary to promote jobs in Derry and then send the biggest investment in ten years off over the mountain? Are you a spy, or are you just a moron?") And then Ellie McGinlay went on air on Radio Mountrose at nine and asked listeners to ring in with their opinions on 'Governor Lundy Schumann' (Lundy is their Benedict Arnold). And, of course, they did. In their hundreds.

They have a point, too. These were very good jobs – software research – and would have been ideal for many of Derry's highly educated and under-utilized computer grads. And in some ways, Ellie's program acts as a release valve for all the crazies – even if she doesn't go a bundle on quality control and wouldn't know a libel if it bit her on her pert little ass. (I'll 'Boston Bungler' her!) She actually rang my office and tried to demand a live interview halfway through her show. It was the only time I laughed all day.

Thank God for Bowtie. He isolated the source of the problem by mid-morning – a greasy little fixer called 'Darkly' Barkley, who'd scared the new American company away from Derry by demanding a mill-and-a-half 'hello money' up front for various interested parties.

To be honest, there are Barkleys in every town and we have to deal with them if we want to do business. They disguise themselves as consultants, but in reality, they're bagmen for politicians and property owners. And they're essential if you want to iron out planning problems quickly, sort out security and personnel issues, neuter union officials and generally get the wheels oiled.

The problem with our Mr Barkley was that he wasn't subtle enough; and he was too greedy. His Belfast counterpart only asked for a mill (all pay-offs are hidden in the land-purchasing fees, if you were wondering), and he was cute enough *not* to invoke the name of a leading paramilitary in his opening gambit.

I've summoned Barkley to a meeting here on Friday; he tried to put me off, but Tommy warned him he'd never get another American cent if he didn't show. It'll just be a dressing down for now, though; the jobs are long gone. Belfast will have them tied up tighter than a fat girl's thong.

My problem – and it's one faced by every single stratum of government in the North – is that I can't take a leak without applying to seven different departments for permission.

Seriously, to make – or reverse – any decision here, you have to go through local planners, local pols, regional planners, regional pols, Stormont planners and Stormont pols, before the colonial British governor

– who goes by the very democratic title of Secretary of State – decides to do whatever he damn well wants.

Okay, that's not entirely accurate, but the supreme authority still lies with London. So, what I learnt today is, if I want anything done, I'm going to have to lean on people there. Mr Barkley, in the meantime, will continue to pillage his ten per cent from the scraps that Belfast (and London) throw this way, just as Big Al did in Chicago in the '20s.

Chris, as you'll expect, wasn't thrilled about being dragged into my mess by the media. For all her gentleness, she's got that inner steel you'll find in women who've risen to the top very quickly. But she didn't blame me – not for an instant. She knows how the politics work here and just advised me to keep my head down and wait for the clouds to clear. She's threatening to sue the *Standard* for their entirely made-up claims and wants it publicly known that no-one has ever been anything but fully satisfied with her brand of, ah, friendship. Though, personally, I'm not so sure how we'd go about proving it in court.

That's not to say I got off the hook entirely. When I called to see her this evening, not having shaved for two days, Chris just shook her head and said, "No way." She then went to her bathroom, produced a plastic razor and said, "Either it goes, or you're on the couch for the night, Dave-boy." But I, being a wise guy, stormed off – and am now sitting alone drinking Scotch and crying to my daddy.

Actually, she rang five minutes ago, just to make sure I'm okay. She understands the pressure and has forgiven me entirely. What a girl.

I'm starting to feel that this one might be too good for me, and she certainly demands I suit up for her and bring my best game. Plus, there's always the added bonus of proving Ellie McGinlay wrong.

Give all my love to Mom – and tell her I'll webcam soon.

So long and slán
Your loving son
David

          Schumann's Shoemakers, Boston

Dear David

It was lovely to meet Chris on the webcam the other night. I tried four times explaining to your mother that it was your new girlfriend, but the poor soul got it into her head we were watching *Ugly Betty* on the portable TV. And I have to admit, Chris bears more than a passing resemblance to Salma Hayek. (If you fell into the river, you'd come up with a beautiful woman in your mouth, never mind a salmon.) Your mom, as I've been telling you, has been getting even worse since her eyes deteriorated. It mightn't do any harm if you were to get a quick trip home to see her sometime soon, while she still remembers who you are.

I know you think I'm nosey, but I'd like to hear a bit more about Chris. I'm seventy-two and am running out of hope that I'll ever meet my grandchildren – but it'd be nice to get a bead on their mother. (How about that for a bit of old-school guilt?) I appreciate, though, that you're still at that stage in your friendship with Chris when most of what you're finding out about her is not for my ears. But as soon as the steam clears off the windows, you might let me know what (if any) long-term plans you have.

I think Chris has it wrong, though, about you laying low and licking your wounds for a while. Politically and professionally, you have to rise and lay low all those before you – before they sense weakness and try to kill you off.

First, I advise taking out Mr Barkley as a warning to those who would follow him. Remember, you have all the aces, no matter how well connected he thinks he is. You're never going to catch him mid-shakedown – it seems he's far too skilled for that. So instead, just start taking an interest in him. But be cute about it. Get your people to make requests about his tax status and his bank accounts, without specifying why. When he resists, as he will, it becomes a federal matter. So you investigate him and follow his money. Track his spending versus his declared income. Monitor his mail, computers and email. Talk to the banks, see what sort of debts he has – if he needs money for a company. Then slowly start to squeeze him. Let him find he can't borrow any more money – and start to foreclose on his loans. I imagine he's asset rich, houses, property etc, so freeze his assets and make sure he can't offload them.

And then, finally, just as he's for the long walk off the high bridge, throw him a bone. Offer him a one-off deal: "You work for me now, kid, for nothing – if you ever want to work again." He'll probably still cream off a slice to pay his bills, but you'll never get a day's bother with him again.

Your problem to date is that you're hoping to get by on your charm alone – you're too well mannered. You're complaining about having no authority when, in reality, you're the single most influential person in the district. You are the American government. You are the American money. And the American money goes where it wants and calls the shots when it gets there. It's not a matter of you leaning on people: you *tell* them what to do. Put aside all notions of fairness in your mindset: you're the boss, so start acting like him.

While you're domesticating Barkley (I estimate it'll take less than a month to break the little SOB), you need to launch a massive PR offensive. Remember your Juvenal – find some bread and organize a circus. Give the public something new to focus on. When Sally Fritz ditched you the day before prom, you could have been the laughing stock of school. But instead, your Uncle Ernie fixed you up with that nice girl who tends bar at his Gentlemen's Club. She turned every head in the place – and that was before you got her onto the dance floor. You left the place a hero. (In retrospect, though, Ernie might have warned us she was a stripper.)

So get back out there, admit your mistake, and start running the game again.

Don't for one minute think your drug problem is over, either. Smugglers are the same as businessmen the world over. They'll be stung by their loss and try to make their money back early. It would be a good time to tempt them into making a rash move.

Back in the late 1920s, a couple of the coffeehouses Old Poppy and Joey K were running in Southie took a hit. And the boys needed to get back in the hooch business very quickly before their clients all blinded themselves down in Mickey Drain-Cleaner's. So the pair of them and a couple of pals headed up through Vermont in four trucks to pick up a consignment over the border in Montreal.

When they got to Canada, however, their contact there, French Pete, was a bit edgy – couldn't quite look them in the eye. A slower man wouldn't have picked up on this; after all, these were dangerous times, and they were all risking a stretch in Sing Sing . . . or possibly worse. But Old Poppy's bells started ringing when he asked Pete for 10% discount – twice what he normally gave them – and he agreed. They were being set up.

So instead of driving the trucks back home along the main road as they normally did, Old Poppy persuaded Joey K to park half their load in a warehouse they owned outside Montreal. Then he and one of their buddies drove the rest of the load down through Canada to Kingston, where, at dead of night, they crossed the lake back into the States on a rickety old private ferry.

Joey and the other driver drove the empty trucks back down through Vermont. And the crafty G-Men waited until they were south of Manchester before hitting them.

Boy, were they shocked when they opened the trucks and found nothing but mountain air! Almost as shocked as French Pete was when the boys went back a week later, pinned him to a table and demanded two free truckloads for their trouble. (Though that story about Old Poppy and the fishing knife is much exaggerated. Pete went on to father two more kids.)

The cops, like yourselves, had decided to hit the selling point – in this case the coffeehouses – so they could follow the guys and find out what routes and personnel they were using. They already knew French Pete was the supplier – but the difference was they'd little interest in him, because what he was doing was legit in Canada. So they just threatened him with a visit from the Mounties and the Canadian tax people if he didn't play along.

Anyway, what I'm saying is these guys are well aware they're being watched, so don't expect to catch them quite so easily the next time. The real problem is that they're too scared to stop – they've got it into their heads that the world is about to run out of money, so they're stockpiling all they can.

We see it here every day: crime is the only growth industry. Apart from shoe repairing, that is. We took on two new staff last week – a machine operator and an office girl. All of a sudden, people are waking up to the fact that shoes aren't disposable items, and that you can get your favorite pair fixed for about a quarter the price of a new set. And don't worry; I've warned the new girl all about Ernie.

Talk to you over the weekend. Give me a call after the BU-Harvard game and I'll fill you in on how we kicked their Brahmin asses.

All our love
Pop and Mom

Whitman House, Derry

Dear Mayor Boyce

I would like to take this opportunity to confirm yesterday's announcement that a senior representative of the US Administration will visit Mountrose in early May. He (or she) will officially open the new extension to the Dunsuffrin pharmaceutical plant, as announced by me yesterday, which will create approximately 400 new jobs for the region.

It was highly premature of the media to speculate that the President himself will be present, although he is scheduled to travel to the Middle East that same month. But as part of the visit, America's number one hip-hop band, the Dirty Big Dogs, have agreed to come and play a free concert in Mountrose Park.

I will furnish you with further details as and when they become available.

Yours sincerely
David Schumann

COVER NOTE

Monty

I don't know who's more pissed off: Belfast, because they're not getting the circus, or Ellie McGinlay, because she has to choke back so much humble pie. She was actually at Tommy's house (to watch the *Scrubs* relay) when I got the confirmation call. And I couldn't resist telling her. Her face went redder than your dinner-date's Wonderbra.

Derry, of course, will reap a big dividend from the announcement as well. I'd imagine three quarters of the new jobs will be filled from the city; it's an easy commute, just seven miles. I've arranged for our Visitor to give a speech at Guildhall Square in Derry – from the exact same spot where General Mark Clark took the salute from the US Marine Corps as they were setting off for Normandy on D-Day. So politically, the city is in the loop as well.

As soon as our Visitor is wrapped up here, Air Force One will fly directly on to London, pausing only momentarily to empty the toilet traps out over Belfast.

Chris, fair play to her, had no problem letting me make the Dunsuffrin jobs announcement. I sorted out the planning issue that had been delaying them in just four minutes. Or rather Darkly Barkley did. He made one phone call and the eighty-five objections disappeared into the air.

In fairness to Mr Barkley, he is a very intelligent sort of man and knew from the second his credit card was declined how this was going to go. I didn't even have to raise my voice. Tommy tells me he's from a line of crooked businessmen – his uncle, 'Sparkly' Barkley, was chief accountant for the Boys and a self-styled property magnate, before his mistress shot him. His brother, 'King Size', the former jockey, then took up the reins (see what I did there?) before he, too, had his black little heart shot out by a scorned woman. Darkly has now inherited the farm and, like the dead relatives, has been given an apt nickname to boot. He is as dark and conniving a man as you will ever meet – the man who stands outside the brothel offering to sell you your photo back. And I now own him.

As I said, Chris gave me the honor of sticking this one in the win column – though it was as much to silence Ellie as to help me. Chris is a very tolerant person and fights with no-one. (Apart from me, maybe. But as I've explained before, a slap on the mouth is just how a Latina woman does foreplay.) Mostly, though, she's a very gentle soul. She could never sack a worker: instead, she gets her personnel people to do it, or maybe Chad Scarpa. She'll always try to see the best in people. But Ellie is the one person she truly hates. She loathes her. When I ask her why, however, she can never put her finger on it, just says she's a "sneaky bitch".

I can't see it, myself; there's no real side to Ellie. She hits you head on. And when she does hit you, it's generally done with righteous, honest anger. I find her show compulsive listening now; there is nothing as satisfying as hearing her debunking hypocrites on a daily basis. As long as you're not her target *du jour*.

The concert was also Chris's idea. Well, I came up with the gig bit, she supplied the act. Her brother's the road manager with the Dirty Big Dogs – they all grew up together in Houston – and when I offered to pay the expenses, he got the guys to waive their fee, so we can hold a freebie. The boys are gigging in Dublin later that week (assuming their singer gets his bail conditions extended), so it couldn't have fallen better.

Your no-show at the poker last Saturday didn't go unnoticed, by the way, you filthy old tart you. If you think the three of us are going to alibi you while you play Tickle Me Elmo with some twinkie who'd get you banged up in twelve different states, you're very much mistaken. Next time you stand us up, we'll simply call your wife and ask her what's keeping you.

And yes, there is a certain amount of jealousy here. Tommy Bowtie says by all rights you should be paying alimony to three different women, just like he does. (And none of them would as much as blow into his ear.) Ed reckons you're only trying to compensate for your receding hairline, widening midriff and chronic midlife flatulence. Ed also says to tell you that he has never needed to look at any woman other than his wife and that the best wine improves with age (you lucky, lucky bastard, you).

I, naturally, smiled and said nothing. But I'm warning you now, Monty – unlike last Saturday night, this will not have a happy ending for you. Women don't like being played, and as soon your wife meets your 'niece' – and trust me, it will happen – they will find another use for that nightstick Ed lent you. And it will not be pleasant.

Consider yourself warned!

Now, I'm away off for some non-marital fun of my own. We can swap notes over the weekend.

Dave

URGENT UPDATE

Police Headquarters, Derry

Dear Mr Schumann

Further to our conversation last night, I can now confirm, as we suspected, that the tablets found in the most recent young victim's jeans contained traces of ketamine. The dosage would not have been enough to incapacitate or otherwise harm 98% of the population, but given Mary McDarragh's history of allergies, it was sufficient to produce a violent seizure when combined with the MDMA and other adulterants in the tablet.

Medical staff at Altnagelvin Hospital estimate that the victim ingested eight tablets – all with the tell-tale St Andrew's Cross marking – before collapsing. Nurses were alerted to the remaining pills when one of Ms McDarragh's friends attempted to remove them from her clothing, surreptitiously, in the A&E ward. This person has since been helping us with our inquiries, and we have made one further arrest – a Mountrose youth named John-Joe McGownie.

Ms McDarragh, who is sixteen, and not seventeen as reported in today's *Derry Standard*, is currently on a life-support machine and is described as being in an 'extremely critical condition'.

The media are already linking this incident to the three previous incidents, including the previous fatality, in Mountrose. And they are not wrong.

Your network of contacts has been of great assistance to us in the past, Mr Envoy. If there is anything relevant that you should become aware of through your channels, please inform me as soon as possible.

Yours
Chief Superintendent Edward O'Conway

COVER NOTE

Dave

I'm reluctant to write down that the poor girl is a goner, but they're just waiting on a sister to come back from holiday in Spain before they turn off the machines.

Mary's father, if you're not aware of it, is Darragh McDarragh, the developer who built Rose Gardens, that massive new private housing estate in Mountrose. He's a big pal of Tommy B's. From what our man tells me, he's already gunning for revenge. And I don't mean figuratively. Mr McGownie is a lucky boy he's locked up safe in one of my cells.

The bad lads will be happy to let McGownie take the fall this time. He'll do a year, or eighteen months max, for small-time supplying (he's still only seventeen and clearly hasn't made a bean out of it), and he's far too afraid to talk. Kitty O'Carty has already read him the mantra: do nothing, say nothing and sign nothing.

Totally off the record, it looks as if you're going to have to remove your little camera from Dr Diaz's boudoir and re-install it in the canteen, my friend. Two deaths in one little town in a year is just too many – and if we don't get a handle on it soon, my Belfast bosses will draft in some crack drugs unit from the 'capital' whose specialism is taking a bad situation and making it worse.

You were right, by the way. It didn't take Nero and his cohorts five minutes to set up another pipeline into the town. Bowtie reckons they're handling the Derry connection themselves now, as Nero has been seen twice at the airport in recent weeks (though, significantly, not as a traveller). My own best guess is that he's tied in somehow with a couple of defunct republicans who head over to Glasgow every two weeks for Celtic matches. They'd be far too cute to bring the stuff home themselves – they know we're watching them. But up to 5,000 people from these shores head over to Celtic Park for these games and we can't monitor them all.

The added complication in all of this is the damn festival you're running in May. What on earth possessed you to recruit the Dirty Big Dogs? Their singer has eight separate convictions for pill popping. Did you ever stop for a minute to consider what sort of people they might attract to their concerts? And I know, I know, it was Chris's idea, and she's been an angel to us over the last few weeks. But contrary to what you've been telling us on poker night, the brain is the biggest organ in your body – so start using it proportionately.

The sad truth in all of this is that we always get a lot more bother from drunks at big events like this than from the 'Eckie' freaks. I guarantee you that any assaults we'll have to deal with at this concert will be drink related. Alcohol kills a thousand times more people in Ireland a year than pills do and lays waste to ten times as many lives again. But no-one's going to do a damn thing about it, because we all use it. And the government earns so much money from it. So come the day of the gig, we'll spend about fifty grand in police man-hours declaring war on a bunch of heavily sedated tablet users, while the off-licences and bars will schlep up rocket fuel to thousands of rowdy troublemakers who are going to vomit all over our streets and then throw rocks at us on the way home.

For that reason, I'm tempted to ignore the party line and let it slip (maybe to Ellie McGinlay) that Mary's convulsion was down *not* to the drug, but to what it was cut with. The Policing Board will blow a collective fuse, but I'm back off down South to the Guards at the end of the year, so they can go shit in their hats. On the continent, they erect tents to detect contaminants in tablets and honest to God, I'd almost set up one myself here.

I'm off back over to the hospital now to tell a man whose daughter is about to die that I'm revoking his shotgun licence. They never tell you about days like this in the brochures – they wouldn't get a single recruit.

See you at the weekend.

Ed

PS You'll never guess who was stopped for speeding by our boys in Traffic last night? With a very pretty young girl in the passenger seat to boot! Okay, it was his nine-year-old daughter, but it should be worth about twenty minutes' entertainment at the poker on Saturday night. That man, by the way, is begging to get caught – he's just too damn proud of himself.

Whitman House, Derry

Dear Pop

It was the saddest funeral I've ever been at. They buried Mary McDarragh in her 'Sweet Sixteen' dress, but when

I saw her laid out in the coffin, I'd have sworn she was five years younger. Same for her classmates. They lined up, in school uniform, outside the chapel to provide a guard of honor at the door – and the principal had ordered no make-up. So they stood, like the frightened, pasty-white little children they are, baffled and heartbroken by what had happened. Not one of them looked more than twelve years old.

As for the music, the choral arrangements inside the church would have drawn a tear from a New York critic. Derry people always boast they're the most musical on the planet, and up to now, I'd always put it down to pub talk. Today, I know exactly what they mean. The soloist – an eighteen-year-old girl from Mary's school – would fill Carnegie Hall. They actually ruled her out of the British version of *Pop Idol* this year because they reckon they've already had too many finalists from this part of the world. They might talk tough here, Pop, but they all sing like angels, they really do.

Typically, it rained in the cemetery, which is the windiest place I've ever been, including Chicago in mid-winter. If you can bear the breeze, it's up on a high hillside overlooking the river and has one of the finest views you'll get of the city. And there was more music there, too – a haunting piped rendition of *Danny Boy* that echoed long and sad down through the valley.

McDarragh was glad to see me; well, as glad as any father who's just lost a teenage daughter can be. But he knows my appearance will put extra pressure on the police to get a quick result. McGownie, the youth who sold the tablets to Mary, is being held in custody. He could probably get bail if he tried, but Kitty O'Carty has warned him he's going to do a year minimum, so he's as well starting it now – and then getting as far away as possible from Mountrose and McDarragh's un-surrendered shotgun.

The good news, though, is that Chris and Chad, the clever articles, have managed to set up a receiver that can intercept all cell-phone calls made from within the plant. McDarragh and Chris sit on the Town Development Committee together, so she's doubly determined to catch Mr O'Neary and gift-wrap his carcass for her pal. I trust she wasn't speaking literally. Chris, as I've been telling you, can get a bit passionate at times. Though that's not necessarily a bad thing – particularly if you've been a good boy all week . . .

Chad Scarpa, I have to say, is one of the cleverest men I've ever met. I really wish he worked for me. Like Chris, he has a PhD, though his is in computing. He's in his late thirties, but looks much younger, and tells me he actually did his Master's at the university in Derry as an exchange student back in the mid-1990s. Paid his fees by bouncing at a local nightclub: "Guy came at me with a broken bottle on my first night. Poor sap wound up falling on it and cutting himself a second asshole. Full twelve months I was there, no-one ever came at me again."

Chad is pretty certain they're going to try to bring the next batch of stuff in through the airport. Nero, for all his caution, has been surfing the air schedules on his home PC, which Chad, naturally, has tapped. Easiest thing in the world to do, actually. The idiot has a wireless network in his apartment (to let him bring his laptop to bed no doubt), and his security code is his date of birth.

Chad didn't even have to go in the apartment window.

To ensure they don't use a boat route, Ed O'Conway is doubling the police presence at all shipping ports for the next month. The clever boy's not going to make a public announcement; rather, he's going to let the *Derry Standard* find out 'by accident' and then run the 'crackdown' as an exclusive. I know from my own days in the mines that newspapers get far more excited if they uncover 'confidential' information themselves than have a story handed to them with a ribbon around it.

As a reward for all my hard work this week, Chris took me for a trip to Ness Woods, about six miles outside Derry on the Belfast road. And I know we journalists aren't supposed to get swept away by the flowery stuff, but it's listed as one of the 200 most romantic walks in the British Isles, and I could immediately see why.

The ancient woods are set into steep hills, and as you stroll along the mazy, dipping, narrow paths, you get some glorious glimpses of the winding Ness River down below. Then, capping it all, at the source of the river is this spectacular waterfall – one of the highest in the country – which, like our Niagara Falls, has attracted its own peculiar brand of daredevil. Apparently, Shane O'Cahan, an eighteenth-century highwayman (or dissolute young lover, depending on who you're talking to), was being hunted by a posse who trapped him at the top of the waterfall. But rather than handing himself over, or taking his chances in the deadly rapids, young Shane took a few steps back and leapt thirty feet across to the far bank – thus breaking not only the Irish record but also a few world ones to boot. The gap has been known ever since as Shane's Leap, and no, I didn't attempt it – no matter what Chris was promising.

And as a reward for securing the extension for the factory, Chris has been offered a major promotion – but it would mean transferring back to head office in Anchorage. (And yes, that is the same Anchorage as in "Fuck, it's cold here in Alaska.") She was given a couple of months to think it over, but, very sweetly, she asked me how I felt about it. And dammit, I don't know if it was the trees or the waterfall – or the sun setting in the red sky, or the fact I'd been too chicken to do Shane's Leap – but I told her. And, God bless her, she put her hand to my cheek and told me, too.

So in short, when I come back home for Paddy's Day next month, I'll have a passenger in tow. But you'll love her, Pop. This could be the real deal.

I must head on now and get ready for our poker night. Ellie McGinlay is joining the group. Tommy, who's her godfather, on top of everything, insisted she needs to start sitting at the big table. She has agreed to (and understands the repercussions of violating) our only rule: cheat all you want, but what's *said* at the table *stays* at the table. There are nights when you literally have millions of dollars of business being done over the turn of the cards. And Ellie, for all her flaws, is smart enough to realize she'll never get another chance.

I suggested Chris join us, but Tommy reckons he's got the Mountrose and American angles well covered through Monty and me. But he expects Ellie to take over as editor of the *Derry Standard* when Mary Slavin retires next year. And she's still a bit rough round the edges – as you are at twenty-seven. So this is her introduction into 'polite' society. I was worried that we might have to ease up on teasing Monty, but it seems that Ellie's feminism fails her when it comes to his wife, our plasticated mayoress. Indeed, she told Tommy if she were married to Barbie Boyce, she'd run around with teen fluff as well.

I'm enclosing a few pictures of myself and Chris for Mom to look at and show her friends. And I'll bring Chris along for our next webchat as well.

So long and slán
Your loving son
David

Whitman House, Derry

Dear Monty

If a single look could voice a thousand words, your expression when we caught you on Saturday night spoke some of the rudest X-rated dialogue I'll ever hear.

The whole thing was O'Conway's idea. He got two of his traffic cops to 'inspect' Heidi Hotbottom's cell phone when they were doing motor-tax checks on the bridge last week. They quickly swiped her number from her address book and gave it to me. And I must now confess I passed it on to Chad Scarpa, who took all of eight minutes to rattle me up the cloned SIM card, which allowed Tommy to send you the saucy text messages.

We didn't think we had a hope of convincing you, though. After all, it's not every day that a hairy-arsed middle-aged lawyer tries to impersonate a trainee apprentice beautician with a forty-inch chest and a fifty-point IQ. We did know, however, thanks to your big mouth, that you'd bought her lingerie, so we figured you'd be hoping for a post-Valentine's Day thank you.

– wd u lik me to put on da u no wot 2nt? tee hee. xxxx
of course i wd. cnt wait. tee hee.
– no wot wd mk it reely hot?
wot?
– u put on da same. b reel fun.
no way.
– pls. pls. pls.
no way. im playing cards.
– o cm on. under ur suit. noone will no. ill b a reely bad grl for u after. reely bad.

That sealed it, naturally, just so long as you didn't speak to her on the phone about your intentions. But thankfully, you're too inhibited for phone sex – that whole Irish guilt thing about self-pleasure, again. So instead, you walked into poker night like a man straddling a barbwire fence.

I looked over at Ellie and the pair of us nearly took the giggles on the spot. Then, thankfully, Tommy cracked the joke about you being late as you had to leave your girlfriend to her lemonade-tasting class, and we got all our laughs out.

We still had to get you to reveal the baby-doll, though, which is where Ellie – and your schoolboy obsession with ogling fresh mammary glands – came into the equation.

We waited until near the end, as we wanted you to

relax and forget about your situation. And sure enough, you did. And as we headed into the last hour, you were comfortably in the lead. Then, in what normally would have been the second-last hand of the night, Ed dealt you the four kings. He's been practicing all week, and you never suspected a thing.

Ellie stayed in, and the rest of us folded. You decided, naturally, to raise her and buy out the pot. She tried to borrow chips from me, Ed and Tommy, but we all refused. House rules.

Ellie, however, was wearing a low-cut chemise, no real bra – just a little string holster – and you just couldn't resist it: "I'll give you fifty credit against that fine silk top."

"No way, Monty. This chemise cost a hundred quid. Tell you what, though. My blouse against your Charvet shirt."

"Done." And you reached over to shake her hand, grinning like the cat that got the booby juice.

And it was at that precise moment you realized what we'd done. Maybe it was our silence, or maybe it was the glint in Ellie's eye. But you knew. And the blood just drained right out of your face. Ellie didn't even have to produce her four aces. With two solitary words, the only printable one being 'bastards', you stood up, took off your jacket, pulled off your tie, then ripped the shirt off and threw it over the table . . . And just so you know, it takes a real man to pull off a pink bodice – and, darling, I'm not sure you've got what it takes.

Oh, and Tommy made copies of the video of it for all of us. Which means you're now buying the beer and peanuts for the table until the day you die. And probably after.

I think we'll keep Ellie at the poker – she fits right in and distracts you just enough to give the rest of us a chance. She even had the grace to forgive me over the Belfast jobs disaster. "I've watched you play cards," she told me at the end of the night. "You come off as this wide-eyed American sap, but no-one ever bluffs you twice. And you never forget – you'll do them next time."

Anyhow, the point of this letter is not just to gloat, but also to let you know that it looks as if our plan is on for next Saturday night, which means the poker's postponed until Sunday.

See you then, and in the meantime, wrap up warm.

Dave

Liars' Row, Dunavady

<u>PRIVATE</u>

Dave

Just further to our bit of fun with the mayor on Saturday past, please do not tell anyone at Dunsuffrin about the incident – even your good friend Dr Diaz. I know Chad got you the SIM card, but it'd be best to keep this one to ourselves.

It's not that our friend doesn't deserve to be publicly ridiculed: I haven't seen anyone behave so stupidly since one of my clients left his mistress's address on his wife's sat-nav.

It's only by the grace of God that Monty isn't now sporting a reverse Prince Albert and barbells through both nipples as you and Ellie were proposing. But I still think it's important that this stays at the table. Not to put too fine a point on it, that sort of information is so juicy that Dunsuffrin, even Chris, couldn't help using it if they needed it.

As you're well aware, there are many different ways to own a man. Most people, as you Americans worked out long ago, you just buy. You find out their price, pay it and they're yours for as long as you need them. The first thing the English did when they were colonising Ireland was to buy the local chieftain. In India, they bought the rajas. Saved millions on fighting the natives. Your banks do it all the time, too. They pay junior executives ridiculously high salaries so they get accustomed to the money and then they threaten to fire them unless they go out and rob the public blind for them.

Sometimes, though, money isn't enough, and one of the legacies of the recent Troubles here is that the Irish in particular tend to resist direct bribes. But Big Brother will always find something. For example, if your child is sick, or your teenager is looking for a place at a good college, all of a sudden you're looking for a Godfather. However, there will always, always be payback. And six months later, you have to fix up Sonny so his mother can look at him . . .

Another method to make a small boy behave, as any parent will tell you, is to take his toys – which is why the Assets Recovery Agency became so popular. There isn't a person alive who can answer honestly if you ask them to show receipts for every penny they've spent for the last ten years. And how they paid tax on it. And no judge is going to accept that you won the money for your new Hummer at the track, even if you are the Taoiseach of Ireland. So we'll take back those keys, please. You used this trick yourself with Darkly Barkley. And I have to say, I was impressed by the cold and ruthless manner that you squeezed him. I didn't think you had it in you.

The quickest way, however, to own a man, and one which we have learned much about over the last fifty years, is blackmail. It's now the favoured weapon of police forces across the world, though I like to think our own Northern Irish constabulary set a very high bar when it came to using extortion to 'keep the peace'. In a nutshell, it boiled down to this: tell me who whacked Lord Lucan and I'll not charge you with eight counts of flashing.

My real fear is if Dunsuffrin ever heard of Monty's dalliances, they would immediately say to him, "Cut our ground rent by thirty per cent – or we'll tell teacher." And Monty would have to find a way to do it.

It's not personal, kid. As a great man once said – it's only business. So keep it closed.

Tommy

PS Be at my house on Saturday night at 8.00pm. The post-match flight's due in at 9.30pm, so we'll want to be there in plenty of time.

Whitman House, Derry

Dear Pop

You know by now that a suitcase of 35,000 tabs was seized, one of the biggest ever hauls in this part of the world. But we very nearly blew it this time – or rather, the cops did. Thank God, Ed O'Conway was there.

It was Chad who got us started. On Friday morning past he was reviewing the previous night's canteen tapes and listening uninterestedly to Nero's soccer monologue to his two pals. Then, without breaking breath, Nero glanced over his shoulder and quickly slipped in, "Teddy Duffy was carrying a twenty-seven-inch Samsonite Cruiseair case, colored silver..." before recommencing with his opinions on the Chelsea team's defense.

It was quite amazing that Chad spotted it. At least, according to him it was, as he's not allowed to show us the tapes anymore because of some damn Human Rights law. But it was enough.

Teddy Duffy – or to give him his official title, Senator Tadhg Ó Dúfaigh – is a Donegal politician and diehard Celtic fan, who flies across every two weeks to Glasgow to the games. Like many boosters, he generally stays a couple of nights at the new Coliseum Hotel before the game – sometimes with his wife, sometimes with a hired-in girlfriend – and then jets back home directly afterwards.

Now, Fat Teddy is no more a drug dealer than Uncle Ernie is a back-row high-kicker at the Folies Bergère. What he is, however, is a big bag of hot wind who is too high and mighty to carry his own suitcase even the shortest of distances. And this means that last Saturday evening, it was the easiest thing in the world for a pal of Nero's – an ex-gunman turned gangster – to make the switch before Teddy checked out of the hotel.

Result: Fat Teddy carries home 150 grand's worth of illegal narcotics in the replica case, while little Tommy Terrorist schleps back a couple of extra-large suits and Teddy's well-worn underwear. At absolutely no risk.

We decided not to clue Teddy in on the grounds that there are more brains in a yellow hat. But thanks to Chad's tip-off, Ed O'Conway's men were able to follow the line the whole way to the hotel – and got pictures of the whole episode to boot.

The problems started at the other side of the Irish Sea, back in Derry. We'd cut a deal with Chris that, if at all possible, we'd arrest Nero and his cohorts this time. She doesn't care so much about where the stuff is coming from, she just wants the bad lads out of her factory – and out of Mountrose – pronto. But the Derry Special Branch were very keen on the gunman – a guy called Barry Bruskin, aka 'Barry Bang Bang', on account of his shorthand method of dispute settling.

They hadn't realized his involvement at all, right up until he marched up to the porter's office at the Coliseum with the claim ticket for a case identical to Fat Teddy's. And they resolved to scoop him immediately after the switchback, which they assumed would happen shortly after the plane touched down in Derry.

They were correct. In Derry, Bruskin stood right at the mouth of the airport carousel to lift Teddy's case, which he'd marked with a red piece of tape, thus making sure Teddy carried the replica through customs. (Tommy Bowtie and I were watching on the TVs in the security office with Ed.) Neither of the men was stopped at the desk on Ed's instructions. Though it would be interesting to find out if Barry Bang Bang had known the lock number to Teddy's case. I'd bet my last dollar he had.

As soon as they got into the foyer, Bruskin politely approached the senator to tell him he'd got the wrong case. And Teddy gave a big shit-eating shrug and apologized gracefully, commenting that this was the third damn time he'd done this.

But the second the cases were switched, two Branch men immediately got up from different parts of the hall and started making for Barry. They were about twenty feet away from their oblivious target when they suddenly pulled up short with very shocked looks on their faces. Like a man on the other end of their earpieces had warned them that their jobs were on the line if they didn't fucking well stop in their tracks. We want to follow this to the end. Besides, as Ed said later, if we'd been caught allowing an Irish senator to be used as a dupe, every one of us would have wound up in jail. Even him.

So instead, four of Ed's own CID (plain-clothes) men tailed Bruskin to his car, then followed him, in two cars, all the way out to Mountrose. Our main fear was that he might head across the border to Donegal, where we had no jurisdiction. But happily, he drove right to a laneway adjacent to John Hawkson's house, where he deposited the case into a black garbage can.

One of the cop cars stayed near the house while the other followed Bruskin back into Derry. Within two minutes, Hawkson, accompanied by McDowd, had furtively opened the back door, and the pair made their way to the bin. Ed momentarily thought of having the two men lifted there but at the last second decided to hold out for Nero as well.

And his judgment proved to be spot on, as the two boys quickly stuffed the suitcase into a small Ford van and drove rapidly to Nero's apartment three blocks across the little town. Ed had a snatch team on standby at Mountrose Station, and they were there within two minutes – just in time to find the three boys sitting at the kitchen table weighing bags of pills on a set of electronic scales.

They didn't so much as flinch when the boys burst in the door. Nero simply turned to Hawkson, shook his head slowly and said, "Some fucker's talking." And the trio slowly stood at attention for their body searches. They weren't going to give the plain-clothes guys the pleasure of a free slap at them on top of losing their stash.

By that stage, Ed, Tommy and myself had made our way back to Ed's office in Derry. And we were still there drinking from a celebratory bottle of Black Bush when the boys were brought in for processing. They all asked for Kitty O'Carty, who instructed them to do 'no-comment' interviews. The police here aren't allowed to listen in on defense lawyers' conversations with their clients but they are allowed to keep the cameras running in the interrogation rooms. So we got to see Nero asking Kitty how long he was likely to serve, and her holding up five fingers.

All in all, a good day. We got rid of Mountrose's three biggest hoods and we now have a shot at closing down the North's dirtiest paramilitary cell. Bruskin is convinced he's in the clear – it's obviously an in-house Mountrose tout – and is just about dumb enough to return to his normal business within weeks.

So Dick Tracy saves the world again. And, as in all the best detective stories, the girl was grateful. Really grateful. But enough of that for the minute. After all, you are my father.

I'll buzz you tomorrow night on the webcam with the update. About 7.00pm your time, to make sure Mom's at her best.

So long and slán
Your loving son
David

Police Headquarters, Derry

Dear Mr Schumann

Just to confirm that the tablets on Saturday night were of identical chemical composition to those recovered from the pockets of the late Ms McDarragh. The consignment had been adulterated with both veterinary ketamine and ephedrine, which can, in a very small percentage of the population, bring on fatal seizures.

Further to your other inquiry, I can also confirm that police have now withdrawn their opposition to bail for Mr McGownie. His lawyer Ms O'Carty argued that any perceived threat against her client was now minimal, though he is not permitted to stay in Mountrose or visit the locale other than for schooling.

Yours sincerely
Edward O'Conway, Chief Superintendent

COVER NOTE

Dave

I wasn't at all happy with John-Joe being allowed to walk until I got my hands on old McDarragh's shotgun. I still think JJ's a silly boy, and he's going to get one hell of a hammering from Mary's schoolfriends. My own son's in that class, by the way, and they can't believe their luck. One broken rib for every tablet she took is the word on the street. Hope they've the sense not to post the thing on YouTube.

As regards anything more serious, though, I doubt it. Nero and his crew know well that John-Joe didn't rat them out. They don't gossip about their runs, and he'd no access other than a weekly hello to Hawkson to collect his packages and pay the rent.

Significantly, no-one has made any approaches to Barry Bang Bang yet. We've been watching him like a hawk. At the very least you'd expect someone, somewhere, to ask him a few questions. But nothing so far. He's either so well connected he's beyond suspicion

– or he's going to be found toes-up in a Donegal field before the end of the week. I know what I'm praying for, but our Special Branch crew are already talking in terms of a sting operation to trap him. They've got it in their heads that he's the brains of the operation – God love their wit.

You'll also be glad to hear that I've managed to part-mollify Mayor Monty, and he's dropped the Mountrose Council objection to your festival in May. Like myself, he was genuinely worried about the nature of the band. That, and he still hasn't got over you exposing his underwear fetish.

But given that the Dirty Big Dogs have agreed to our extensive security arrangements (we get to search all their gear with a fine-tooth comb as soon as they land in the country), and that the blood has now returned to Monty's brain, I think you can go ahead with the booking arrangements.

For all that, we're still not in the clear entirely. Monty's vowed never to come back to the poker – he thinks we were disrespectful. As if! And apparently your note to him merely rubbed salt in the rope burns. I'll leave it to you and your New England charm to sort this one out. Maybe something bottle shaped might help. Oh, and tell Ellie to drop all the cross-dressing jokes she's been storing up.

Talking of whom, glad to see you're on better terms with her now – as long as we stay off the subject of Chris. Wonder is there a little jealousy there on Ellie's part? I know, I know, it's more of a brother-sister rapport you have with her – you've made that very clear. But women are odd creatures, Dave. And I speak as an expert, who has lived with the same one for thirty years and still knows nothing about the workings of her mind.

Anyway, I must head on now and try to stop Special Branch from launching an air raid on Barry Bang Bang's council bungalow. See you at the game on Saturday night. And settle things with Monty before he does himself an injury stomping off in those high heels.

Ed

Whitman House, Derry

Dear Mayor Boyce

Many thanks to you and your council for acceding to the consulate's request to host a festival at Mountrose Park in early May (date to be confirmed). We appreciate the concerns you had and will endeavor to assist you in all security-related matters in and around the event. We are also happy to meet your fee for use of the park amenity and for the seating and stage provision.

We are confident the festival will strengthen links between our two countries, and that the accompanying official visit will give due international prominence to your exemplary borough.

Yours sincerely
David Schumann

COVER NOTE

Monty

Attached, find a bottle of Hennessy's Cognac Paradis, which I had flown in from Boston specially for you by way of apology. I've never seen it anywhere in Ireland. And just in case you think it's not sufficient, let me be vulgarly American and tell you that one solitary pint of this stuff retails for about £500, give or take. If God cried tears, they'd taste like this.

Plus, Tommy Bowtie has made us all promise to lay off the teasing. So stop huffing in the corner and come back to the game, you big girl. I mean, you big manly man, you.

Seriously, Monty, where are you going to find four other suckers willing to hand you over their hard-earned money week after week? And it's not as if you didn't walk right into this mess yourself. We've been warning you for weeks that you're two steps from a fall – so be grateful that it was your friends who tripped you up and then caught you.

That's the great thing about friends: unlike your enemies, who are cruel because they hate you, we're entitled to be cruel because we love you. And we take no joy in your pain (or at least very little). For what it's worth, the story never left the table – and there never was a video. One of us suggested it (I'll not embarrass her by naming her), but I wouldn't allow it.

And besides, your reappearance will add that little frisson of excitement, raising, as it does, the delicious prospect of your revenge. Who will be your first target

– and how will you choose to humiliate her?

Also, many thanks for removing your objections to the Dogs. Darkly Barkley tells me that his opposite number in Belfast was ready to offer them a big payday up there if the Mountrose deal was cancelled – anything to poke Derry in the eye.

What's more, Chris is mightily relieved and has promised that not only will you be on the podium inside the factory during the May visit, you'll also get to do the introductory speech. And that's pretty much your re-election in the bag. Unless, of course, you revert to type . . .

Chris is coming back to Boston with me for a visit next month to meet the folks. I can't wait to show her off – she'll stop the traffic there. I might even introduce her to Uncle Ernie if we can coax him back into his Hannibal Lecter cage first.

She knows that I'm a bit uptight about her visiting, as it's probably the last chance I'll ever get to introduce my mother to a girl she might remember. But she's been very relaxed about it – putting no pressure on me at all. That's the thing about intelligent women (as you might someday find out yourself), they can read our minds. You know the way you can never bluff Ellie at the cards (indeed, none of us can)? Chris can see right through me the exact same way. If Ellie's little cheeks didn't light up when she gets a good hand, you'd never stand a chance.

Now, come back to us on Saturday night and I'll stand you a few bottles of Stella.

Dave

URGENT

Dave

Damn, damn, damn. It's exactly as we feared. The body they pulled from the bottom of the quarry this afternoon was John-Joe McGownie. And to answer your next question, no, it's not suicide.

He'd a six-inch hole in his belly – the type you get if someone stands two feet away from you with a sawn-off shotgun.

Say a prayer old McDarragh has a good alibi. I don't think his wife could cope.

Tommy

Tommy Bowtie writes:

The poor, poor boy. We all knew it was going to happen, but it was the last thing any of us needed. Dave was already so gung-ho about our smuggling successes, a dead body was always going to fire up his old reporter's instincts. Trying to get him to focus on his day job now was going to be very difficult . . .

MARCH

Whitman House, Derry

CONFIDENTIAL

Dear Mr Ambassador

Further to our telephone conversation last night, I think it is essential that we now move immediately to assuage concerns that there might have been a 'mainstream' paramilitary link to the shooting of Mr McGownie in Mountrose.

The PSNI and Special Branch have given our consulate their total guarantee that there was no involvement from traditional republicans – pro-Sinn Féin IRA personnel, whether past, present, retired or freelance. It is vital that this message goes out both in Britain and in the wider world, for the sake of political – and hence economic – stability.

I am happy to make the statement on your behalf from here, although I think it would carry more authority emanating centrally and from your lips. And yes, it is a broad sweeping statement, but the police are satisfied that there was no official republican sanction for this shooting – even at the lowest level. Not so much as a wink.

For your personal information alone, may I advise you that one line of investigation being pursued by the PSNI is that dissidents may have carried out the murder to embarrass Sinn Féin. These dissidents are particularly keen to garner support in hard-line republican areas where there is some discontent at high crime levels and the perceived failure of the IRA to intervene. I doubt this myself and have already made it clear I will stop all American visas forever for any and all dissident supporters, should this prove to be true.

Much more likely (and again, this is for your eyes alone) is the possibility that Mr McGownie was killed by the father of drugs victim Mary McDarragh. Mr McDarragh publicly stated at her funeral that he'd avenge her death, and the police now believe he may somehow have secured another gun.

Mr McDarragh was, naturally, questioned about the incident at length but said nothing at interview, other than to admit that he was glad McGownie was dead and that he was sorry he hadn't done it himself. He refused point blank to account for his whereabouts at the time of the killing on the grounds that the police never once asked him to account for his whereabouts on the night of his daughter's death.

Shortly after his arrest, however, three of McDarragh's friends voluntarily gave statements asserting he was playing pool with them in Dunavady, fifteen miles away from Mountrose Quarry, when McGownie met his end. They insist that he didn't leave their company at any stage of the evening. The police know this is a big fat pile of BS, but they are reluctant to call the three witnesses out-and-out liars, given that one is the politician Shay Gallagher MP, the second is a bank manager, and the third is the lawyer, my own friend Tommy McGinlay.

Off the record, when I asked Tommy why he had alibied McDarragh, he told me: "Two reasons. One, I really don't think he killed the boy. But, two, I also have a sixteen-year-old daughter. And I think it's important for little boy drug dealers to learn how us dads feel about them."

So Mr McDarragh was released without charge and,

given the huge level of support for him in the community and local press ('We're with you, Darragh' – *Derry Standard* headline), the police are unlikely to re-arrest him, even if he hands over the still-smoking shotgun and his blood-spattered boots. Sometimes, Mr Ambassador, even the best people here behave like hillbillies.

One other possibility being examined by the police is that the triggerman may have been a maverick dissident republican who works as a runner for a local drugs gang (yes, I know, it makes my head hurt as well). This man, Barry Bruskin (alias Barry Bang Bang) may have gotten it into his psychopathic head that McGownie was responsible for a number of recent drugs seizures in Mountrose, whether through his own carelessness or by direct informing. So the theory is that Bang Bang 'banged' him as a message to others. Again, I'm not convinced – but the police are keeping a very tight eye on Mr Bruskin, and I'll report back when I have more.

I am confident that this incident is a complete one-off, and that it should have no impact on the state visit here in May. This was the first shooting in Mountrose for almost twenty years, the time when Mayor Monty's uncle took a bullet in the thigh exiting his neighbor's bedroom window. And given what we know, it is extremely unlikely that there will be any reprisals. There were fewer than twenty people at McGownie's funeral, so I really don't expect any retribution from that corner.

Looking forward to seeing you at the St Patrick's Day celebrations in Washington later in the month.

Yours sincerely
David Schumann

Police Headquarters, Derry

Dear Mr Schumann

Your office asked us to keep you apprised of any developments, so I wish to inform you that we have this afternoon arrested a fourteen-year-old youth in connection with the McGownie murder.

Given the age of the youth, we will be making no further public comment at this stage.

Yours sincerely
Edward O'Conway, Chief Superintendent

COVER NOTE

Dave

You'll no doubt know through the jungle drums by now that we've lifted McDarragh's son Rossa. Our search teams recovered what they're pretty certain is the murder weapon in a massive gorse thicket about a mile from the quarry. And while there's no DNA on the weapon at all, there were two small scraps of wool recovered from a gorse bush, which are a perfect match for a couple of strands missing from young Rossa's Aran sweater. At the very least, he's in the frame for dumping the gun.

Truth is, I'd love to let it all slide but I'm under immense pressure to get a skull here – and not just from the higher-ups who want this whole thing in a pretty little parcel before the visit. Ellie McGinlay and her bleeding heart started a real backlash today. She announced on her programme that if we're going to execute teenagers who sell lethal products, we should maybe start with the shop assistants who peddle cigarettes and bar workers who sell whiskey. The Holy Rosary brigade are already out and supporting her. And as I've said before, logically, it's a hard argument to whack.

I'm very aware (just in case you believe I'm as idiotic as the *Standard* would have you think) that young Rossa could well be the victim of a stitch-up. And two strands of wool and no alibi (same line as the father) do not make a case. I await the revelation that he was playing a football match witnessed by all 5,000 Mountrosians at the time of the shooting. Interestingly, though, McDarragh the Younger told his school counsellor that he would 'sort out' Mr McGownie, a fact which she'd already reported to the Head. And last year he won the County Derry Junior Clay Pigeon championships, thus answering your next question.

I'm still harbouring a notion that it's Bang Bang, though, and was hoping you might be able to provide me with some of the help I'm not allowed to ask you for, and you're not allowed to give me, but which has proved so valuable in the past. I'll talk to you about it on Saturday night at the poker – maybe afterwards, as otherwise I could risk the McGinlays coming at me from both sides.

Well done in getting Monty back in harness, by the way. But watch your back – he'll not rest until your photo's on the front page of the London *Times*, resplendent in peep-hole bra and crotchless pants. You have been warned.

Ed

Whitman House, Derry

<u>CONFIDENTIAL</u>

Dear Monty

Just to advise you that word is going to break this week about another big jobs announcement for Belfast. A thousand jobs are to be created there by the US medical company, Zonk-Zonk Sleeping Pills. Nothing we could do about this one really – we didn't have the immediately ready floor space they needed. But we're (I'm) going to catch a bit of flak for failing to enhance the 'pharmaceutical cluster' your council has been dreaming of ever since you were lucky enough to land Dunsuffrin.

For the record, I didn't even get a chance to argue the toss for the region – it was as good as sewn up before I got here. Darkly Barkley tells me that the developers in Belfast then sealed the deal by handing Zonk-Zonk's soon-to-be-divorced vice-president a $500,000 kickback in used notes.

Belfast, unfortunately, is still light years ahead of us in terms of commercial enterprise, nuance and outright corruption. Derry is too moral for its own good and still entertains nineteenth-century notions of fairness and justice when it comes to trade. Belfast, like all successful capitals, knows the only moral worth talking about in business is to close the deal at all costs.

More positive news is that my good friend Dr Diaz has organized top-level meetings for the Derry and Mountrose delegations with four multinationals during our visit to the US later in the month. She's already pitched the CEOs the virtues of the area – the educated workforce, low production/labor costs, strong currency, low tax and start-up grants – and reckons your charm (or *plámás*, as you call it) should be enough to do the rest. So take it easy on the beer while we're away, my friend – I want us to come home smelling of roses, not barroom carpet.

Chris, the angel, is going to help us offset the nuisance of the Zonk-Zonk revelation by recruiting an additional 100 R&D staff at her plant next week. And she's also agreed to sponsor an anti-drugs program in all schools in Mountrose and Derry. (I'm not allowed to tell you what my forfeit was for that one.)

Other good news, again totally off the record, is that it looks like McDarragh Senior is in the clear over McGownie. Chad, as you're aware, has been helping Ed (ie the cops) through the mire on this one, in a totally private capacity. And without giving too much away, he's established beyond doubt that McDarragh wasn't in Mountrose for most of the night of the shooting. The poor man was where he's been every evening for the past three weeks: grieving hopelessly at his daughter's grave in Derry while his wife tries to coax him home.

Still not sure where the son was. Though, again, his direct involvement is looking less likely. Privately accessed computer records seem to indicate that Rossa was online and active at the time of McGownie's death. Though Rossa was dumb enough to write down his innermost feelings about his sister's 'killer' and then post the same to every crazy who'd listen. So he's still not off the suspects list yet.

I tend to agree with Ellie's suggestion that we should let Nero out for a while and keep tabs on him. He's due to apply for bail this week and, given his father's cancer, we could legitimately release him and not the others without raising too much suspicion. I think all of us want the bad guy here to be Bang Bang, and it would be just perfect if Mr O'Neary could lead us to his door.

Ellie's told me to warn you, by the way, not to so much as dream of exacting any of the revenge on her you've been muttering about. Quote unquote, "I'll bury him in the same quarry as John-Joe if he tries anything." Given you're too scared of either Tommy or Ed to try anything on them, can I just add my sentiments to those of Ellie's and assure you, that while I fully respect your need to get even, I am the guy with the keys to the red phone.

See you on Saturday night – dress casual (and heterosexually).

Dave

Whitman House, Derry

Dear Pop

Things are slowly but surely getting back to a more acceptable pace after a couple of weeks of sudden death, murder and political upheaval. I'm hoping this marks a change of direction for us, and not just some comic relief in a Shakespeare tragedy.

The bad news is that it looks like John-Joe McGownie's killer is going to get away scot-free. At least for the time being.

The Derry court released Nero on Monday morning, after Ed O'Conway had spent the weekend setting up a thirty-strong surveillance team to keep tabs on him. Unfortunately, our man wasn't half a mile down the Mountrose road before he spotted the tail. He pulled his car into a lay-by almost immediately, flagged down the unmarked cop cars following him and told the surprised Branch men to take him back to jail.

At the police station, Ed asked him would he not have preferred to spend some time with his dying father. To which Nero replied, "The idea was for me to go out and bury my dad – not the other way about. And trust me, Mr O'Conway, thanks to your escort, that's how this one was going to end."

For all I hate what Nero did before, I have to admire his intelligence. And he's also telling us, in no uncertain terms, that McGownie wasn't nutted by a fourteen-year-old schoolboy.

Surprisingly, though, on that score, our man Chad still has his doubts about Rossa McDarragh. He's convinced Rossa is bright enough to set up pre-generated postings from his computer to appear as if he were at his bedroom desk when he could have been out roaming the quarry. And he's pressing Ed to get an order to seize all the family's hardware.

The only other major suspect, Barry Bang Bang, has gone to ground like the hunted animal he is. And Ed and Chad both reckon it's going to be very difficult to pin anything on him as the days wear on. If you don't get your man in the first forty-eight hours, apparently, your chances of securing a conviction at any stage drop by about half.

Despite the security crackdown, there's still no shortage of tablets making their way into the town. There were four arrests at the weekend for possession and two for supply. But at least the message about the dangers of overdosing seems to be getting through. And I notice that a couple of posters to the town's 'alternative scene' website are signing themselves 'Stick to five and stay alive' – an allusion to their in-house safe levels.

My other great frustration here is that, not content with keeping all her own cookies for herself, Belfast is still attempting to steal whatever crumbs are left for the rest of us. Some idiot launched a protest at Stormont that no-one east of the Bann had been invited to the four private meetings Chris had set up for Derry with private US investors in Washington. (How they got to hear of them, I'll never know.) Result was, two of the American companies got scared off and have cancelled, whereas the other two have now agreed to meet with both Derry and Belfast delegations. There are days you should be allowed to smack in the mouth anyone who crosses you – and this is one of those days.

Chris is blaming herself and tearing her long, lovely Latin hair out over the mess. Despite her 'legs of steel' image, she's a little insecure when things go wrong. Charmingly neurotic, I tell her – though it's the price you pay for being so well-organized and professional.

Outside the office, too, she has the occasional tendency to doubt herself – which, for me at least, just makes her all the more appealing. How anyone so beautiful, smart and generous could ever be unsure of themselves is beyond me. She actually confessed last night that she had never been offered a promotion in Alaska at all but had dropped a little fib to find out where she stood with me. I'd kind of suspected as much myself, as Chris is never done complaining of the cold here and swears her last remaining ambition is to be living in Florida by the time she's thirty-five. So the Anchorage deal never really rang true. But you can't imagine how thrilled, and flattered, I was to discover that this woman I am so into was so into me right back. I barely even remembered to give her a hard time about lying to me.

Tommy Bowtie reckons I should never have let Belfast muscle in on the meetings, and that I need to get much tougher with them, or at least provide him with the ammunition to do so on my behalf. He and Ellie took me out for a stroll on Lisfannon Strand in Donegal on Sunday afternoon to give me a hard time about American inertia. We walked for three miles along spectacular beaches with coastal views you'd only ever see in Hollywood sea pictures, watching yachts tacking their way across the four-mile Lough Swilly to Rathmullan. I'm aware, of course, that they were selling me the place. Again.

But truth is, they have no need to. I was so entranced by the views that I barely noticed they were spending the entire time bitching at me.

I actually asked to take Chris on the walk, too, but Ellie vetoed it on the grounds that Chris is pursuing her own agenda, and I mine. I know they don't like one another but I've explained to Chris that Ellie is no threat to her, and that it is possible for men to have platonic friendships with women. "Maybe if you're a homosexual it is," she retorted. So I wisely left Chris to her overtime.

I'll catch up with you soon on the webcam. Big hello to Mom and tell her I'm really looking forward to seeing her in a week's time.

So long and slán
Your loving son
David

Schumann's Shoemakers, Boston

Dear David

Many apologies for your mother's behavior on the webcam last night with Chris – I think I've finally worked out what it's about. She'd gotten it into her head that we were watching *House* and became convinced that Chris was Cuddy, House's hard-nosed boss whom she hates with a passion: "All he does is save lives, Samuel, and she treats him like the wipings of her ass." So then when 'Cuddy' started talking to her from the 'television' and calling her Mrs Schumann, Mom lost all reason.

Please tell Chris how sorry I am and assure her that I'll have it all sorted out by the time the pair of you land here.

Rest assured, for my money, Chris is a diamond. But I think it's time, perhaps, that you and her both backed away a little from the murder inquiry. You've got carried away in the excitement. As long as it was factory business, it directly concerned Chris, and you could make the argument for your Batman and Robin double act. Now, though, you've become little more than garbage men for the cops – doing the dirty jobs they can't or won't do themselves. And I'm a little concerned about some of the detection methods you're using. As you'll remember, I never had any time for LBJ, but he had a point when he said that every man should know that his conversations, correspondence and personal life were private. Start sticking cameras on people twenty-four hours a day and you might stamp out crime. But each and every one of us will end up in jail.

Call me an old fool, but I don't think any of your three suspects killed the young fellow McGownie. None of them stood to gain anything.

As a father, I know how it feels when someone harms your child – your immediate instinct is to strike right back. But then your better angels kick in, and you realize that your long-term responsibilities to the child – or surviving children in McDarragh's case – include demonstrating your core morality and your respect for due process and conflict resolution. (And yes, I should never have waved that baseball bat in Louis Marzo's face after Lou Junior bust your eye with it. But at least I didn't fire a starting pistol in his ear like your grandfather did to Francie Doherty's old man when Francie knocked out one of my teeth thirty years previously.)

McDarragh didn't kill McGownie, because that would have made the father as bad a guy as the dealer was. And I'll bet your mother's heart medication that he'd warned young Rossa not to touch him, either – and had him watched night and day to boot. And a fourteen-year-old boy, even a very smart one, would have messed up that shooting so many ways that he might as well have written his name and address on the corpse. There's no way he could have done it without leaving a trace. And the strands of wool they found on the bushes were put there by some clever policeman trying to get himself a stripe. As sure as eggs and cops are rotten.

And your terrorist friend, Barry Bang Bang, is way too cute to blow the most successful smuggling pipeline since Moses parted the Red Sea by stiffing a seventeen-year-old kid who knows nothing about nobody. Bang Bang isn't the brains of the outfit, either. He's a hired hand, who in this case did his job well and lifted his check. He had no beef with anyone. Find out who's paying Bang Bang, though, and you'll get your shooter.

It doesn't surprise me, either, that there's still an unhealthy supply of those damn happy tablets making their way into the town. Smugglers, because of the nature of their jobs, will always have contingency plans ready.

Back in the Roaring Twenties, Old Poppy and Joey K once fitted a fleet of timber trucks with false fuel tanks, which allowed them to carry fifty gallons of whiskey a visit out of Montreal. They had about a month of very profitable trips before a café owner asked Poppy where he was getting this high-quality hooch from. He then insisted on knowing how it was being brought in – after all, he was paying top dollar for it. And Poppy knew that very second that the game was up. The guy was obviously being squeezed by the gendarmes. So he told him – off the record.

The next trip out of Canada, Poppy filled all the dummy tanks with gasoline. And sure enough, when he was stopped on the way home, the *federales* went directly for the whiskey. But instead of getting a mouthful of Quebec Maple, the taster got a belly-load of full-leaded petrol. Meantime, Joey K had skipped across to Ontario and bought a whole batch of Hiram Walker's finest rye, which he snuck back across the Detroit River in his cousin's motorboat when everyone was busy back in Montreal.

The trick, as all boy scouts know, is to be prepared. And the men you're dealing with get up early in the morning – just like your old granddaddy did.

Can't wait to see you both next week and take Chris on the Freedom Trail tour.

'Fraid your mother's insisting on separate rooms, dementia or no dementia.

But don't panic, she sleeps like a baby, thanks to the new pills the doc gave her. I, on the other hand, have the ears of a bat . . .

All our love
Pop and Mom

Police Headquarters, Derry

Dear Mr Schumann

Further to our conversation this morning, I can now confirm that we have instigated internal disciplinary action against a Scenes-of-Crime officer, who may have inadvertently transferred fibres close to the site of a recent weapons find. A file has also been sent to the Police Ombudsman.

Yours sincerely
Edward O'Conway, Chief Superintendent

COVER NOTE

Dave

As soon as you mentioned it, I knew who'd done it. Harry York has been angling for an inspector's cap for three years now and must have thought he'd netted it for sure this time. He tried to brazen it out, of course, and even suggested that young Rossa may have been in the area innocently on another date. But when I hypothesised that maybe he, Harry, could have brushed up against Rossa and accidentally transplanted the woollen threads to the bush, he leapt on the possibility just that bit too quickly. So we did him.

Anyhow, thanks to Chad, we can now put Rossa out of the picture entirely. He's been through the PC with a fine-tooth comb and is certain it was being operated on live when McGownie was being operated on dead.

But despite what you were telling me, McDarragh Senior is still a possible fit. He could have driven from the cemetery to the quarry and back, all within a reasonable time frame. It's unlikely – but there's a fine line between grief and anger, and I'm still not sure what side I'd be on if it were me.

The better news is that our old pal Mr Bruskin, aka

Barry Bang Bang, is on his travels again. He's heading back over to Glasgow this weekend, so I have a team of sixteen deployed to watch him like a hawk. If he so much as puts his hand in his pocket, we'll do him for lewd behaviour.

Depending on what's happening in Scotland, I might be a little late for the cards on Saturday night. I agree entirely with Tommy's proposal that we ban mobile phones from the table, à la *Michael Clayton*. Between your office and Monty's totty, we barely got a single uninterrupted hand last time out.

Slán go fóill
Ed

Liars' Row, Dunavady

<u>EYES ONLY: HFC</u>

Dave

Tremendous catch this evening, second in a month. You've a real talent for this, or rather, your old man does.

Ed's just off the phone to me. The bad lads spotted the police tail on Bang Bang at the airport just as you said they would. So they reckoned they were safe to leave him as the decoy and bring their stash home on the ferry. And they weren't expecting the forty extra coppers at Larne Port to search every single bag coming off the Sunday afternoon boat. Tens of thousands of tablets and two warm bodies in the cells – that's a handsome haul.

The guys they scooped are again low level, unfortunately. Too young to be ex-players, too stupid to realise they're patsies, and too frightened to say anything. Kitty O'Carty has already been in and worked her magic on them. So the short answer is, we're never going to find out who's paying them.

Ed is actually bursting to lift Kitty herself and have Chad trawl through her files and computers. But despite her clients, I think she's pretty straight. That's why they go to her. Dirty lawyers are two a penny, but the smarter punters know that if someone's crooked *for* you, it's odds on that somewhere down the line they're going to be crooked *against* you. So, ignore everything you've ever heard: honesty *can* be profitable in this profession.

I'll talk to you Tuesday morning, and we'll get the agenda sorted out for the trip. Well done on the cards last night, by the way. Your first win. Told you it'd be better now we're all phone free.

Tommy

Town Hall, Mountrose

<u>PRIVATE AND CONFIDENTIAL</u>

Dear Dave

Great result yesterday – just heard about it on the morning news. Almost £200,000 worth of stuff. And all down to a classic double bluff. Let them think you're buying the dupe, and then crease them when they're trying to sneak in the side door. If your poker playing improves at a similar rate, as it seems to be doing, I'll have to find other ways of stealing money.

See you at the airport on Wednesday morning – seven sharp.

All the best
Monty

PS Get any interesting text messages recently?

Mountrose Radio FM, Mountrose

PRIVATE PRIVATE PRIVATE

Dear Dave

Text messages? How cheesy. Would have expected more from you. Maybe a letter? After all, you're becoming renowned for your correspondence.

Then again, perhaps it's cute. And I was forgetting that Chris can break into your computer at the touch of a button (well, Chad can at least), so you're careful what you write there.

If you're serious, give me a ring when you come back from the States and we can talk about this properly. I don't believe you're going to end things with Chris. For a start, I don't think she'd let you.

For the record, I think about you quite a bit as well. And yes, under a certain light, you're almost presentable looking.

But I'm a big girl and I know how these things go. And it was late at night and you'd had a few beers. And I had been looking particularly well that evening at the poker.

Your greatest attribute, though, is that you're straight, so I know you'll call it one way or another when you come back from Boston.

Have a great trip. And yes, I'll miss you, too.

Ellie

PS I've had a tip-off about who might have recruited the lads at the weekend. The downside is I have to go clubbing on Saturday night to meet with the source! The cards are off because of your American trip, so I suppose I'm doing nothing anyway.

Whitman House, Derry

<u>CONFIDENTIAL</u>

Dear Ed

You bastards.

You, Monty and Tommy have landed me in it, and no mistake. And while I'm not normally a man who complains when he's punked, there's something very cruel about your stunt – particularly as it involves innocent parties.

This incident has, unfortunately, made me feel the need to review my friendship with the group and my participation in any of its future events.

I think it's time you brought in another card player for Saturday nights, as I don't intend to return.

Yours
David

PS Never mind me; how could you do this to Ellie?

Police Headquarters, Derry

<u>URGENT</u>

Dave, Dave, Dave

For God's sake, hold your fire and think about this.

All right, I'll admit, Tommy and I knew that Monty was going to clone your phone – that's what the whole Michael Clayton rule was about. We wanted your mobile left at the door so that when Monty left the room to take a pre-arranged call, he was able to snag your SIM and Chad got it copied and back again before the night was over.

But do you seriously think we approved of what Monty did after that? We thought he was going to order us up a crate or two of champagne on your dime, which we'd all guzzle down. And you wouldn't find out that it had been your treat until the bill came.

It was only when Ellie asked Tommy yesterday if you were a bit of a ladies' man that he started to catch on. He then teased it out of her that Monty hadn't mentioned to her that he'd cloned your phone – and at that point, he knew.

Tommy was so annoyed when he heard about the texts that he drove to Mountrose, stormed into Monty's office and slapped the mayor with the flat of his hand across the mouth. For you. He then hit him a second time and told him that one was for Ellie.

He didn't say a thing to Ellie about it, of course – or that she'd been duped by Monty to get at you. For all her tough talking and brutal interviewing style, Ellie's still a softhearted little thing underneath.

The problem is, Monty is so astute and so psychological. It's what makes him a great politician. He sensed a little hankering on Ellie's part, so he decided to mess with both your heads. And he knows that you're such a damn gentleman, you're going to have all sorts of sleepless nights trying to get your way out of this one without either hurting Ellie or letting Chris know.

Part of this, Dave, I have to say, is your own fault for making fun of Monty. He might only be a small-town shyster, but you made him feel like it. And now he's making you pay. So rather than stamping your feet, I'm afraid you're going to have to suck it up – just like Monty did.

There is, of course, an undercurrent to all of this, which you're too smart to miss: you really like Ellie, and it's starting to become obvious. Take it from a clear-sighted old cop.

Now, call home your petted lip, and go off and enjoy the party in America. And come back and play cards with us next week.

We'll sort it all out. Don't worry.

Ed

Liars' Row, Dunavady

<u>HFC</u>

Dear Dave

My sincerest apologies for what happened at the weekend. Our prank got away from us, and I have already spoken quite sharply to Monty about his particular behaviour. We'll talk about it on the trip and work out some sort of explanation for Ellie for the return leg. Probably best to go with the truth, as she's just like her mother, God rest her, and sees right through me. I think Ed's right, though, and you might have a decision to make, sooner rather than later.

Ed also tells me that you're thinking of chucking the poker. Please don't. We need you there, if for no other reason than to remind us that, while our little parish is indeed the centre of the universe, we still have to co-exist with greater forces – like yourself.

To use one of your own sporting analogies, Dave, we know we're little-league hucksters, but you're up there batting with the pros. And we need to learn from you.

By way of atonement, I've managed to organise a meeting with the CEO of Zonk-Zonk Industries for yourself and myself in Boston on Saturday morning. I invited Monty as well, but he's not comfortable taking part in small-group sit downs until he gets his front teeth re-installed (wrestling accident with his kids).

I don't expect anything out of the meeting, to be honest – Belfast has the jobs locked up – but Chad knew the guy's head of security. And you never know, we might just pick up a few outsourcing crumbs.

Two bits of bad news, however. First, the last consignment of pills we got from the ferry were very low quality. They're from the same lab, no doubt, but very weak – which means, of course, the youngsters tend to take a lot more of them. So when the stronger batches come back into town, disaster.

Also, the police in Glasgow have got very angry with Ed over his failure to clue them in on the recent ops. They're starting to take an active interest in the McGownie killing and have demanded access to all our interview notes and forensic reports. It seems they've got their own local favourite for the job but aren't prepared to let us know who it is. Typical copper pissing contest. As my late father always said, boys will be boys and so will middle-aged men.

See you tomorrow on the plane. For some obscure reason, you and I are booked in Business Class while Monty is at the back door of Economy, right beside the toilets. Hope this helps.

Tommy

Irish Embassy, Washington

HFC

Dear Ed

There's only so much green beer a thirty-seven-year-old gut can take, so I've sloped off from the party to drop you a line.

First off, thanks for your letter. I now accept entirely that you and Tommy were (mostly) innocent in the affair, and I appreciate very much your combined efforts at chastising Monty. Tommy told me how you threatened to have the Fraud Squad look at his corporate expenses if he ever tried another stunt like that. And if there's one thing I've learned so far on this trip, it's that Monty is a man who loves a corporate expense. (Though how he's going to justify the $800 in small bills he spent at the Boston Tease Party is beyond me.)

I've been keeping Monty at a distance on this trip, and as you know, Tommy left him out of the Zonk-Zonk meeting today. But despite the whole mess, I can't stay mad at him for much longer. He's just so damn contrite looking and so damn happy when I even acknowledge his presence. He reminds me of a puppy I used to have, who couldn't help peeing all over the floor when he saw you.

The real problem is, as you rightly spotted, I'm a little conflicted. And it's not just the seven green beers talking. When I got that note from Ellie, I panicked – not because I'd been set up, which I knew immediately, but because of the thrill that shot right through me. She likes me, Ed. And much as I want to deny it, I like her, too.

Of course, I also like Chris – as does at least one of my parents. Pop spent the past two days charming the socks off her, though this was as much to mitigate my mother's worst excesses as anything else. God love her, Mom now thinks Chris is Julia Roberts before she quit the streetwalking in *Pretty Woman*. And she treated her with exactly the amount of respect that Jewish mothers have for streetwalkers who are cozying up to their sons. Which is very little indeed.

Chris has been an angel, however, and weathered each and every insult with a smile. Even if she did wince a little when my mother asked her if her breasts were starting to sag.

Chris has also been such a great help networking on this trip, and the two meetings she'd set up for yesterday went brilliantly. The Belfast interlopers didn't even get a look in – the American delegations were too busy looking at my girlfriend's perfectly pert chest. It'll be worth fifty jobs minimum before the month's out.

It's only a matter of time before Dunsuffrin (or some other wide-awake rival) starts putting Chris's talents to better use. She's wasted running a factory in a little town on the edge of the world. Which brings me back to my original problem. The only reason she's going to stick around Derry is for me. My dilemma is: should I be encouraging her to? I really am caught between a rock and two soft places. If it wasn't for the green beer, I don't think I'd get any sleep at all at night.

I had an interesting chat with my father before I left Boston about the much-weakened pills you got stuck with. As you know, Pop's a mine of information about smuggling, thanks to his own family skeletons. He was telling me that his father and Joey K would occasionally 'give one free' to the G-Men, and let them capture small consignments of booze they were moving, on the grounds that it could distract them from the bigger game. ("A dog bites less when he's got food in his belly.") But granddaddy wasn't running a charity, either, so he made sure that any of the stuff seized was at least 80% tap water.

I was telling this to Chad on the webcam last night

– as you know, he stayed behind to look after the store – and he reckons it's quite possible the boys in Glasgow are working off a similar script. And he says it's significant that few of the low-grade tabs seem to have made their way into circulation anywhere – be it Derry, Mountrose or Scotland.

All of the above is, needless to say, HFC (Tommy's in-house code for Highly Confidential).

See you in a couple of days – and thanks again for tossing my nipple back into the pram.

Dave

Schumann's Shoemakers, Boston

Dear David

This should get you pretty much as soon as you land back. If not, you'll already have received my apologies by phone.

All I can say is that I've known your mother sixty years and she'd never, in her right mind, behave like she did to Chris this week. And while it's small consolation to Chris, you and I both know that your mother is so far from her right mind that it's heartbreaking. She has calmed a little since you both left. But between the eyesight and the Alzheimer's, I'm not sure I am able to look after her any more. I might have to think about getting a nurse in.

Chris is a beautiful girl, and she certainly has made you straighten your back. You're dressing better, speaking more clearly, swearing a lot less and, from what Tommy told me, drinking a lot less, too.

I really like Tommy, by the way. He is a good friend to you and promised me that anyone who tries to harm you will have to get through him first. And I believe him – particularly after what he did to Monty's mouth.

Monty is a lovely guy, too, but I wouldn't trust him further than I could throw your Uncle Ernie. He can't stop himself, he has to have the edge on everyone he meets, yourself included. He's the type who will be a great friend as long as he needs you but will drop you quicker than a warm diaper when the stink starts to hit. He also makes a dirty opponent, as you've already experienced, so try not to tick him off again.

For all your talents, you're not a natural political operator, David – you don't have it in you to kill your enemies and move on. Monty does. As, I suspect, does your girlfriend.

Chris, for all her gentleness, is an extremely political animal. I watched her at the Patrick's Day event in Faneuil Hall, and she worked the room like a veteran. She shook every hand, flirted with the men, talked fashion and haircuts with the women, and gave every single person in the room her card. My one concern, and I hate to say this, is that you're never going to be enough for her. No-one is. She doesn't need your approval. To everyone else in that room, you were the big-shot envoy who's about to set Irish-America alight; to her, you're a middle-ranking civil servant, who earns about a fifth of her salary. You see, that's the other thing I noticed at the party: Chris always gravitates to the most important person in the room. Four times she dumped different companions to schmooze with someone with more studs in their collar. In one case, I think she did it halfway through a sentence.

As long as Chris is in Mountrose, you'll remain her number one, as the stark truth is she can't possibly trade up. There's no-one there can top you. And I really do think she is fond of you. But when I mentioned grandchildren – a passing remark made lightly and in jest – the look on her face told it all. It wasn't that she was shocked or horrified, rather, she looked totally surprised at the suggestion, and even a little confused. Like she'd never considered the prospect, not ever. And while I have nothing against career women (your own mother taught school for thirty years), I don't think marriage forms part of Chris's long-term plans at the moment.

If I'm interfering, I'm sorry. But I'm not getting any younger, and it's a parental prerogative. And it sure beats your mother's approach of throwing juice cartons at Chris every time she comes into a room. Also, I'm not sure you're thinking clearly at the moment – you're still at the stage where all you want to do is smell the jasmine oil and watch the steam rising off her naked back. But take it from an old fool, character is important, too, and lasts a lot longer.

I'm disappointed that The Boss won't be able to make the Mountrose trip after all. But you'd been careful not to promise him – and confirming Joe Biden's appearance will soon take the edge off it. Doesn't matter either way as long as the Dirty Big Dogs show up; they're the real money, or so you young folk tell me.

Talking of which, another thought for you. Your smuggling pals are going to start stockpiling very soon for the festival. You've got 60,000 kids coming to town for a three-day event. So if what you tell me is correct, they'll be needing supplies of up to a million pills. And they're not going to leave it all to the last minute. They'll want the stuff stashed a few weeks beforehand, as they know the cops are going to be watching all the land, sea and air routes in the run-up. They're also going to try to set up a distribution network for the concert-goers and will recruit them out of Derry or Glasgow – and not Mountrose, where everybody knows everybody else. So tell Ed to be on the lookout for new faces in town.

I'm sorry I didn't get to meet Ed, by the way. Tommy speaks very highly of him and talked about his strong morality. An unusual thing for a lawyer to comment on, particularly with regard to a copper. But Tommy, for all his dark edges, is a very moral person, too, and clearly sees it in others. Like yourself.

I agree entirely with Ed and Tommy that the shooting had no Scottish angle. This was local, and I think your only hope is to start squeezing Nero in jail. Maybe charge him with directing the killing from his prison cell – see if it's enough to scare him.

Alternatively, let him out again and wait for a few days until he becomes careless. And he will. He has a lot of lost time to make up for and will need the money. Talk to Ed when you get back and give him my best. He sent me a card to say he was sorry he couldn't make it this time but that he'll call in the summer. Make sure he knows he's very welcome.

I'll go now and try to find something nice and safe on the television for your mother and me to watch.

Classic films seem to work best with her, as her long-term memory is still functioning to some degree.

I might have to hold fire on that trip to Ireland next month unless your Auntie Ruth agrees to live in for a week or so. I'll keep you posted.

All our love
Pop and Mom

                                            Whitman House, Derry

<u>HFC</u>

Dear Ed

Thanks for keeping a lid on our mid-air misfortunes. Tommy had to shell out a total of ten big notes (sterling) to assure the cabin crew did likewise. Money, I hasten to add, he will recoup from Monty if he has to shake it out of his still-warm corpse.

I warned Chris not to take Sheila on the trip; the girl, despite her somewhat Rubenesque stature, just can't hold her liquor. Her skirt rises three inches higher with every Screwdriver she knocks back, which meant by the time we hit mid-Atlantic, it was all but over her head. And when you combine that with Monty's inability to turn down any three-course dinner handed to him on a plate, Row E soon resembled feeding time at a very horny zoo.

In fairness, we'd done so well to keep them apart at the various parties and functions we were attending. What we hadn't counted on was that Monty would pay for an upgrade to get the seat beside her on the way home. They still might have gotten away with it if Monty hadn't insisted on a post-coital cigar and set the alarm off in the toilet. And Jeez, who knew that the stewardesses had an emergency key and could pull open the doors so quickly? Euggh. When the pair of them fell out onto the aisle, a wobbling mass of pink legs and other assorted floppy bits, I nearly bit through my plastic fork. It was like a page from a *Joy of Sex* manual written for little fat ugly people.

The pilot was actually going to divert to the Azores or Iceland until Tommy got him squared off, while I had the job of taking the mayor of Mountrose by the ear and leading him to a spare seat at the back of Economy. And no, I did not touch any other part of his body – nor will I ever again.

Tommy nearly had to shell out another grand to buy a cell phone from a fifteen-year-old passenger who naturally, being fifteen, captured the whole thing on video. Luckily, however, the boy's mother intervened and made him delete the file on the spot without a cent changing hands. Though in truth, the boy probably knew in his heart there was no market for it – not anywhere in the world.

Chris, very atypically, was going to fire Sheila on the spot but decided at the last second not to add fuel to the flames. Instead, she told her to see Chad Scarpa first thing in the morning, which had the effect of turning Sheila's complexion sheet white and rendering her completely quiet for the rest of the journey home. Though then again, this might also have been the twelve vodka-oranges.

I rang Monty for a chat about it last night, and while he was hungover and maudlin, he wasn't remotely guilty-sounding.

"You think I enjoy being a middle-aged playboy?" he said. "Fact is, it's all that's left for me. For the past five years, my wife has me consigned to the spare room – and that's where I'll remain until she turfs me out. Which I imagine will coincide exactly with the day and hour she has to stop wearing the mayoress's chain. So I have two years, tops, of living in hell, before I get to spend the rest of my life in poverty and oblivion. I might as well have the odd happy memory to take to my early grave."

I almost felt sorry for him – almost.

Tommy tells me that you've let Nero out again (on compassionate grounds) and this time dropped the tail. It was inspired to get him to wear the electronic tagging device, though. It'll only be a matter of time before he'll get too confident. Then you have him.

He'll have to move soon, too. He's got little or no money since that team of forensic accountants you sent in cleaned out his secret bank accounts and nabbed that very pretty black Hummer he was driving about in. (Let me know when it comes up for auction.) Chris tells me she might be obliged to take him back at the plant, as she's not technically allowed to sack him until he's convicted. And that whizzing sound you can hear is Chad Scarpa searching through employment-law databases for loopholes.

I know I'm not really supposed to say anything to you, but Ellie's source, whom she was supposed to meet somewhere in clubland last weekend, stood her up. All very mysterious. But he's promised to meet her in Dunavady's Pink Paradise Bar on Thursday night. I told her I thought someone was stringing her along, but she just sniffed that there was only one man in her life stringing her along and left it at that.

And yes, we still have to have 'the conversation'. But I'll be damned, Ed, if I know what to do. You're just about the only person I can talk to about this. Pop is too old and, for all his liberal credentials, doesn't really approve of women who work, which means he can't be impartial about Chris. Tommy Bowtie is Ellie's uncle and thinks the sun shines out of the niece's soft little bum. And Monty caused the whole damn mess to begin with. Though whether I should curse him or thank him, I'm still not sure. (And Monty's views on mating rituals are simplistic to say the least.)

And besides all of the above, I trust you, Ed. My father says I should, and he's as good a judge of character as I've ever met. And best of all, you understand women; happily married for thirty years, you're a walking cliché.

I could never say a bad word about Chris, but, in my quietest moments, I know it's going to end the moment one of us is transferred from Derry. It has to. And I'm at the age where I don't want that any more – it's not enough for me. I need a little permanence. But as long as we're both here, I reckon I'm going to remain loyal to her, because, when all is said, it's the least she deserves. And it's no chore, believe me.

So why, then, is this vision of copper-red hair and bottle-green eyes still keeping me awake at night?

I muttered to Ellie that we'd have a full chat on Friday night, so that everything gets sorted out before the poker game on Saturday. That gives me a few days of a stall. How do you think she'll react if I asked her to wait about aimlessly for six months until I get off the pot? Yeah, I didn't think so either. Alternative nights maybe? (It would almost be worth proposing it to watch her beautiful cream face light up red with anger.)

Any thoughts on all of the above would be very welcome. And sure if all else fails, you can always loan me your service revolver and a clip of .38 ammo.

See you on Saturday if not before.

Dave

                                    Police Headquarters, Derry

<u>HFC</u>

Dave

The great thing about life is that if you give it time, it will make most, if not all, of your decisions for you. The trick is not to rush it.

I'm just off the phone from Tommy, and he tells me that each of three multinationals you sat down with in the States last week has already approached him about recruiting Chris for their head offices. You weren't the only guy using that trip as a shop window, my friend.

You might have to stall Ellie for a little while longer, but I think there's a way you can get out of this without losing any friends . . . or indeed, testicles. Just go to Chris now, confront her with what you've heard, then gallantly refuse to stand in her way.

Tell Ellie you need a couple of weeks' breathing space, allowing enough time for Chris to vacate her offices. You should then have a relatively seamless transition and no-one's feelings are going to get hurt.

Chris is so focused on the next phase that she'll suspect nothing – and worry even less. Ellie, likewise, knows it's not a rebound thing and that you're serious. So it's win, win, win. In theory at least.

Life also has its own wicked sense of comedy, so proceed with caution. None of us ever plans to fall out of an aeroplane toilet with their bare arse in the air. But it happens, as well you know.

I really wish you hadn't told me precisely where Ellie was meeting her source tomorrow – or had written it down, at least. I'm now obliged to send out a couple of people to keep an eye on her. Or maybe that's what you wanted all along?

I've got two very pretty twenty-one-year-old cadets (boy-girl) who are the only cops in the station who don't realise they're about to embark on a sordid affair. So I might send them out to the Pink Paradise together for the fun, and to get the balls rolling.

Whoever's there, it won't be Nero. As part of the bail conditions, I demanded a 9.00pm curfew every night. And clever though he is, he's never going to get that tracking device off his ankle without triggering the alarm. He's been good as gold since he got out yesterday, by the way. His only venture outside his father's house (where he has to stay) was to the factory to beg Chris and Chad for his job back. According to Sheila, whom I bumped into last night (and has been partly forgiven, as you know), he was in with them for a full hour. But when he came out, his face was ashen, and he dropped his security fob onto Sheila's desk on his way out the door.

My money's on Bang Bang Bruskin being Deep Throat. Ellie had previous contact with him during his bad-lad days, when he'd come into the station's offices to drop off political statements, condemnations and occasional 'claims of responsibility' for whatever gang of murdering thugs he was working for that week.

Honest to God, he was in so many different republican factions, I was certain he had to be working for us. (He wasn't.)

Bang Bang realises, no doubt, that he's now Number One face in the frame for the McGownie killing, so he'll be looking for Ellie to help clear his name before any deal. He hasn't appeared on the radar at all since the shooting, which makes me certain he's over the border in Donegal. But he might feel safe enough to risk a run across now. And I'm certain Ellie would have contact numbers for him. She should be safe enough; Darkly Barkley owns the Pink Paradise and will give us full access to his CCTV pictures if we need them.

And talking of the devil, Tommy Bowtie says that he's arranged another meeting with Zonk-Zonk at which Mr Barkley is going to make a full and frank apology for his earlier attempt to shake them down. He will also state for the record that he was acting on behalf of no-one but himself. It's part of what Tommy terms the 'Contrition Process'. And the message, he hopes, will go back through Zonk-Zonk to the States that this little parish is cleaning up its act.

I'll go now and track down young Bambi and Humper and hand them out their assignments for tomorrow night. Jesus, I can almost smell the pheromones rising from the locker room. I think we might even hide a camera inside their unmarked car for the journey home, just for the hell of it.

Never trust a copper with brown eyes – or indeed any other coloured eyes!

Slán go fóill
Ed

Town Hall, Mountrose

HFC

Dear Dave

Two things. First, a sincere and overdue apology for my recent behaviour and for my boorish and dismissive attitude to you when you confronted me about it. I am unhappy in my life and acting badly. And I realise that your comments to me are made out of concern and friendship. When all the political bullshit and *plámás*-ing are said and done, you have been always and still are a true friend.

I spend my life pulling strokes and trying to get the edge on other guys who are pulling strokes and trying to get the edge on me. It's so rare to meet a man who will always try to do the right thing because it's the right thing and not because he's working an angle. So thank you for being my friend. And just so you know, I am now four days without alcohol.

Second, I need to talk to you about a possible security leak in our little poker network. A photo of me, which could only have been taken by one of the four of you, has been sent to my computer with a note warning me to be on my best behaviour. I fear it's only the start of something.

You, Tommy and Ed are probably the closest people in the world to me. And Ellie, well, dammit, we've got used to one another and I'd never do her a bit of harm, or she me.

What the hell's going on, Dave? And who's looking to own me?

Monty

Whitman House, Derry

Pop

Damn, damn, damn. Just back from the hospital. It's exactly as we feared. An accidental overdose. She's in a coma with heatstroke and chronic dehydration.

Ten-plus MDMA/ketamine tablets, according to the levels found in her blood. Two more tabs found in her pocket – the doc gave them to Ed for forensics. The CCTV, needless to say, wasn't working – and not a single witness. The place emptied as soon as she fell over. I'm so angry, I think I'm going to kill someone. I'll probably start with Ellie. If she ever wakes up again, that is.

Your loving son
David

Tommy Bowtie writes:

I don't know who was the most stupid: Ellie for arranging the meeting, me for allowing her to go ahead with it, or the police for taking their eye off the ball. One thing was certain, though – Dave's anger didn't come near my own. But unlike him, I knew straightaway that Ellie's coma wasn't self-inflicted. Someone had just tried to kill my niece. And I hadn't been there for her . . .

APRIL
♠

Police Headquarters, Derry

<u>CONFIDENTIAL</u>

Dear Mr Schumann

Contrary to reports in today's papers – *Derry Standard* headline, 'Poisoned!'; *Derry Tribune* lead, 'Was She Spiked?' – there is no evidence that Ms McGinlay's collapse last Thursday night was down to foul play.

Two undercover police officers who were in the Pink Paradise have testified that they had full view of Ms McGinlay while she was in the club and at no time did they see anyone else enter her open booth.

I will be issuing a statement to this end this evening.

Ms McGinlay's condition remains critical but stable in Altnagelvin Hospital. Due to the unusual nature of the incident, police are still investigating and are asking anyone with information to contact detectives at Strand Road.

Yours sincerely
Edward O'Conway, Chief Superintendent

<u>COVER NOTE</u>

<u>HFC</u>

Dave

Sincere apologies. Unfortunately, I have to stick with the official line – as in the attached BS – until I know exactly what the hell happened.

Best we can tell, our two trendy young 'operatives', Lieutenant Bambi and Little Miss Humper, stood out so badly that punters in the club were pointing at them and laughing out loud. So they decided to have a couple of jelly shots to fit in. Then a couple more. Then a couple more. And give them their dues, they even started to dance a little. But no-one was buying it. Then Humper, who is the brains of the outfit, suggested to Bambi that if they really wanted to make it look authentic, they should slip out the back of the club together. She'd heard in Bible College that this is how couples who are bound for hell behave when the demon alcohol possesses them.

They were gone for around twenty minutes or so. And from the smile that's been on young Bambi's face ever since, I can only assume that Humper is a damn thorough method actress. But, of course, they missed the damn conversation inside, if there was one, and no-one else will talk to me, even at the point of a subpoena.

Darkly Barkley, in fairness to him, was so angry with his staff that he fired all four bartenders and both his doormen. But when I asked him why he hadn't sacked the guy in charge of the CCTV he clammed up.

I had to press him hard before he eventually admitted that he hadn't clued the guy in on our need to retain the footage. Apparently they have an in-house rule that when there's any bother in the club at all, the discs are automatically wiped to rule out legal comeback. It was instigated to protect the doormen who sometimes have to do what doormen do to get rid of troublesome punters. So despite all our best intentions there, we've wound up well and truly, ah, in the same position as young Humper.

As regards whether Ellie was spiked or not, I'd bet my eye-teeth she was. But unless she comes round, we're never going to know for certain. And the stubborn fool had publicly stated, just two weeks previously on her radio show, that she didn't think MDMA was any more harmful than alcohol, and that if she could be guaranteed an unadulterated tablet, she might even try it herself.

Which brings me to the other thing we're keeping under wraps.

Traces of strychnine have been found in Ellie's blood stream, along with all the other assorted junk such as ketamine that's used to cut the Ecstasy. Part of me hopes that whoever gave Ellie the tabs had mixed the strychnine in for her personally, and that this batch isn't going to make it into wider circulation. As you know, there's no saying if or when she'll come round again.

I heard you spent the entire night reading to her on Sunday. Tommy was very touched – and even Chris understood. The human touch and voice are very important to coma patients. Apparently, though, they remember everything they're told when they come round – even promises. So, as one friend to another, be very, very careful!

I'll give you a bell when I have more. In the meantime, I'm off to give a, em, stiff lecture to Bambi and Humper about the need for constant vigilance. They're so relieved they're not being disciplined or drummed out of the service that they've forgotten about the bigger picture: I own them both, now and forever.

Yours cynically
Ed

Whitman House, Derry

Dear Pop

Chris, as I was predicting, has decided to leave Derry, albeit a little sooner than I expected. Probably in early May after the concert and Biden visit. A Florida posting, too, if she plays her cards right, so she can get some well-deserved heat in her bones.

She told me over dinner in her place last night, but unlike when she mooted her made-up promotion, there was never any question of me fighting to make her stay – or indeed of her wanting me to.

She's also twigged to my itch for Ellie. Strike that. She told me outright. Truth is, it's been pretty difficult to hide for the last week. But she admitted to me that it was undoubtedly her unwillingness to commit to something a little more long term that had me looking beyond her in the first place.

As I left, we simply hugged like old friends, and she promised me that in her next life she'd hunt me down and chain me to her bedroom wall. But this time I won't have my own key.

I'm so glad it never became boring or, worse again, bitter. It was, as I'm discovering so often with life, just a matter of bad timing. And we handled it more maturely than I could ever have dreamed. Even if Chris did insist on dropping into our goodbyes that redheads are "God's little mistakes". Twice.

And there goes another one. Tell Mom I'm sorry. Though in this case, I don't think she'll be rending any garments.

It also looks like we're going to be losing Chad Scarpa, as Chris put in a big shout for him with her new bosses. He's done eight years here, all told, and needs a new challenge. I suspect also, though I'm not talking with any specific knowledge here, that Chad's connections with a certain government agency won't do him any harm back at home. Ed O'Conway's sure going to miss him, though. And who am I going to get now to make sure that my own 'security staff' aren't monitoring my emails and phone calls?

Chris is still going to sit in on this week's meeting with Zonk-Zonk and reckons we should land up to 100 outsourcing jobs (medical packaging). She referred to it as her going-away present to me – "or at least the only one you can tell anyone about".

I called in to see Ellie on the way back from Chris's – my first guilt-free visit. She looks whiter than God's sheets. The doctor is still refusing to call it one way or the other. Even if she does recover, her kidneys are going to be in a bad way. And that's before you start on the brain.

I read to her from the paper for about an hour – including the death notices, which she never misses. She actually does a skit on her show now and again called The Honest Obituarist: *Beattie McDoherty, colorful and much-loved grandaunt, died in Valley View Nursing Home on Tuesday aged ninety. She will be sadly missed.*

Translation: *Beattie McDoherty, frustrated battleaxe and closet alcoholic, died alone, raving and shouting at orderlies.* Not very tasteful, granted, but it can be quite funny as long as it's not you.

As I was leaving, Tommy and Ed were arriving, the former still far too angry, the latter trying to mollify him. Tommy is Ellie's only living relative: her mother died in childbirth, and her father, Tommy's brother, took himself out with drink ten years later. And Tommy reared her like one of his own, "only better", as he says himself.

They're convinced Bruskin was Ellie's meet and are tracking him via his cell phone, so that as soon as he steps back across the border, they'll lift him. They only found his cell number two days ago when Chad managed to crack into Ellie's home computer, but they now have a full-time read on him. I just pray for Bang Bang that Ed gets him before Tommy.

Anyhow, I'm going to scoot back over to the hospital and tell Ellie some more of my basketball stories. Maybe it's just me, but she seems to like them. Her face seems to relax – or maybe it's true what Tommy says, and the body's got its own extra-deep coma mechanism.

So long and slán
Your loving son
David

Schumann's Shoemakers, Boston

Dear David

Much better news on your mother as I was telling you on the webchat. Indeed, you saw it for yourself: she knew who you were and remarked on how tired you look. The switch in medication has made all the difference. And yes, she may have also sympathized about how your "prostitute" girlfriend left you, but the doctor says it takes about a week for the drug to kick in fully.

Improvement or not, I think it's wisest to postpone my visit, maybe until August. I'm not sure Aunt Ruth is up to looking after both Mom and Uncle Ernie, especially since your mother still has the court order insisting that Ernie keeps 100 yards away from her at all times. (Man, was he ploughed – funniest Hanukkah ever.)

Physically, Ernie could probably stay in his pool hut and your mother in their guest room, a distance of ninety-one yards. But there's always the danger he'd jump the fence again. And it's not fair on Ruthie at her stage in life to be trawling through strip clubs looking for a seventy-six-year-old schoolboy.

I'm glad to hear Ellie is battling on. And well done on leaking to the newspapers how her drink was spiked – it'll allow her to retain a little dignity when she wakes up. And note, David, how I said "when" not "if". Life, as you will realize as you get older, is all about faith.

Whoever slipped her the Mickey Finn is a very polished operator. They would have had to wait until she crashed, or just before, to plant the tablets in her pocket. My own best guess, for what it's worth, is that it's an inside man. And I tend to agree with Mayor Monty that someone close to your inner circle is rotten.

The time Old Poppy was caught with two lousy cases of Canadian Club in his Southie café, he was always convinced it was the driver who'd brought them in who squealed, Tony Bigmouth. Poppy did six months in Sing Sing over that – you couldn't believe how indignant he was. (Though in his heart, he knew the stretch was down to the scores of much bigger shipments they never caught him with.) But anyhow, it wasn't until Tony died in the 1950s and Poppy refused to go to the funeral that Joey K confessed that he himself had turned Poppy in. The G-Men had caught Joey with a marked bottle and threatened him with serious embarrassment unless he gave them a decent scalp. And Joey, of course, was very prominent at that stage and couldn't risk the exposure, so he handed them Poppy instead. All of which explains why Joey's grandchildren dock their yachts off Hyannis every summer, whereas Poppy's grandkids get to scrape the *drek* off their hulls.

The lesson for you in this is that big money will always do what it has to to protect itself. You've been telling me for months now how you domesticated Darkly Barkley. I'm not so sure. That type is always a lot cleverer than they let you believe – they let you underestimate them. Like Joey K, they convince you that they're the lapdog and you're the lord and master, but as soon as your back's turned, they're running round sniffing any loose crotch that'll have them. You've got far too complacent about Barkley and talk far too freely in front of him.

Your other problem is that, like Old Poppy, you're far too close to the story to spot the big lie. For one thing, Darkly's lying about the CCTV videos. Not about destroying them – they're gone – but about ever wanting to retain them in the first place. Think about it; he had one job to do, and what happened? He destroyed the evidence. A very plausible excuse he gave you, too – incriminating himself to a misdemeanor to cover up a hardcore felony.

But start shaking this tree, Dave, and you never know what might drop. Though be very careful not to shake too hard, as you don't want elephants landing on your head. And by elephants I mean Bang Bang and Nero, who are working so close with Darkly on this you can barely see the join. It's a triumvirate as old as time itself: the moneyman, the hitman and the director of operations.

It still doesn't tell you where the stuff is coming from. And with less than four weeks before your big festival, you've barely time to bless yourself. (Boy, I just love dropping in your Irish expressions when I meet Rabbi Silberman.) Ultimately, Darkly is the key to the supply line. Bang Bang hasn't the political skill to handle information like that whereas, I'd imagine, Nero actively doesn't want to know, as it could treble his sentence. So squeeze Mr Barkley just right and he'll give up his BFF quicker than Joey K sold Old Poppy down the Hudson River.

Also, keep an eye on Monty. His blackmailer, and I'm assuming it's Darkly, isn't looking for money, just his silence. And it's possible Monty isn't even aware what he's supposed to keep schtum about. Yet. But, come the time, I hope he has the guts, and the sense, to tell you.

Give me a webcall as soon as you've any news on Ellie – if not before. I have all my Catholic customers over here lighting candles for her.

All our love
Pop and Mom

Police Headquarters, Derry

<u>CONFIDENTIAL</u>

Dear Mr Schumann

Further to your inquiry, I can indeed confirm that police this afternoon arrested Mr Dennis O'Neary (aka Nero) for suspected violations of his bail conditions. He was attended in the station by Ms Katherine O'Carty, solicitor, and after questioning was released.

Yours sincerely
Edward O'Conway, Chief Superintendent

<u>COVER NOTE</u>

<u>HFC</u>

Dave

Chad Scarpa is a genius. I'd almost ask the Board to double his salary so that he could stay here and work for me.

He figured out that Nero had contrived this device, using tinfoil and a relay transmitter, which allowed him to cheat his electronic leg iron. Apparently, there was some data on it on a specialist code-cracking website. So sure enough, when we raided Nero this morning, there were six packs of tinfoil sitting on the countertop of his father's kitchen. Not enough to nail him, though – and we couldn't find the circuit cutters or transmitter. But it puts him back in the frame for Ellie. He was certainly at least supervising Bang Bang, who wouldn't have the brains to prepare a Mickey Finn himself (or indeed refuse one, seeing as you're having one yourself).

Best of all, when we had Nero in the station, we offered him coffee. Being Nero, he insisted on one from the machine – and also asked for a Mars Bar. But Chad, who knows Nero's eating habits from the plant, had second-guessed our man and had a perfectly re-wrapped Mars ready with a miniature tracking device hidden inside.

Sadly, it's only good for forty-eight hours, as is the way of these things. But we can probably rinse and repeat a couple of times at least. If it comes off, it'll allow us to follow him as he sets up his distribution network for next month.

And you're right; we'll hold fire on Darkly until after tomorrow's meeting. But as soon as Zonk-Zonk are gone, his ass is mine. In a totally heterosexual way, that is.

Talk to you tomorrow night.

Ed

Whitman House, Derry

Dear Mayor Boyce

Thank you for facilitating yesterday's meeting with Zonk-Zonk Industries at Mountrose Town Hall. It was an extremely positive discussion, which I'm convinced will result in many benefits for all parties involved.

Yours sincerely
David Schumann

COVER NOTE

HFC

Well played, Monty.

Between yourself spinning the beauty of Mountrose Valley and the outlying glens, and Chris singing the virtues of the educated and committed (ie non-union) workforce, the Zonk-Zonk people wound up kicking themselves for going with Belfast.

The days of us heading Stateside and returning to Ireland with our pockets full of jobs for everyone are over, and despite the very positive noises we got, the other firms were more interested in Chris than in Derry. So it's a major coup that we got ourselves on the Zonk-Zonk radar. They were so impressed that CEO Eric Zweithand rang from the plane to say we've bagged ourselves the 100 outsourcing jobs, which the Veep can announce during his visit here next month.

Interestingly, Zweithand didn't believe a word of the Darkly apology: "Snake-eyed little bastard. Thinks I'm going to forget how he tried to shake me down for a mill and a half. But thanks for showing us you've now got a rope round his neck." And he laughed out loud when I told him we'd arrested Mr Barkley on the Town

Hall steps just as soon as the Zonk-Zonk limo had disappeared up the Derry Road. "Pity you didn't let me in on it," said Zweithand. "We could have all kicked the shit out of him together."

Darkly, naturally, didn't say a word when Ed put the cuffs on him – just asked for Kitty O'Carty. And apparently, things have been just as silent down at the station. He flinched a little when Ed told him he'd seized his computers and had an order for his phone records. He knows it's only a matter of hours before we tie him to Nero. Chad is already merrily hacking his way through Darkly's assorted codes and passwords, even as I write.

They're also going to check the Pink Paradise's CCTV discs to see if there are any ghost images left on them by mistake. Truth is, we're never going to find enough hard evidence to snare Barkley – he's far too smart ever to write anything down. And the chances of us getting a conviction are about the same as Bill Clinton's are of hiring another twenty-three-year-old intern. But Darkly's going to be so busy answering questions from forensic accountants for the next five years, the only drugs he'll be importing from now on will be the Nurofen he needs for the constant pain in his ass.

The bad news, though, is that Nero has skipped. He's crossed the border into Donegal, according to his tracking device – the internal one, that is. The still-functioning leg iron is beeping away from the guest room in his father's house. Better news, for us at least, is that Nero's father has, at tops, a week left to live. And I'd bet my private video collection that the son will come back to say goodbye.

With Darkly and Nero out of the picture, the gang's only hope of making their bucks out of the festival is Bang Bang. And it's possible he could set up shop himself with a unit of four to six other hard men. But that entails someone else shipping the stash into Mountrose, and Ed doesn't think the Glasgow end would take that risk. Not with so many feathers in the air.

I'm still concerned, though. Drugs are as much a part of big concerts now as T-shirts, scalpers and ten-dollar burgers. And a 60,000-strong, three-day gig is too big an opportunity to miss for our hard-working entrepreneurs. It could be worth a million sterling to them. The question is, though, at what cost to the rest of us?

The great thing about a crisis is that it allows us to put pettiness behind us. I was sitting in Ellie's private room last night when Chris came in with a book of poetry which she thought I might want to read for Ellie.

I'm never done being surprised at the capacity women have to forgive, forget and move on. Chris told me her only problem with Ellie had been rivalry over me, which, she said, the two of them had spotted a lot earlier than I did. But she now wants her to get better, as I'm going to need someone to look after me.

Tommy Bowtie wasn't thrilled at Chris visiting – he's very antsy about having anyone there that might scare Ellie witless if she should wake up. But he calmed down when he saw the book. I had a look at the poetry; empowering women's stuff – *Still I Rise*, and all that. Right up Ellie's alley. Now all I need is for a nurse to read it to her . . .

Still no real change in Ellie's condition, though the doctor says her internal organs are strengthening. A good sign, yes, but not worth a damn if she doesn't wake up.

Tommy only ever leaves her side now when either myself or Ed do a shift, which means he's running his office from her room. He got himself a fold-up cot, which lets him nap there, too, so I've volunteered to do a night or two as well. And I think Ed might do Sunday. You're very welcome to fill in any time as well, but you have to promise never to use it as an alibi. Tommy reckons that could only bring bad luck.

Poker, as you're aware, remains suspended until Ellie's back at the table.

I'm glad to hear you're well on your way to your thirty-day chip. I honestly don't think you have so much of an alcohol problem as you have an unhappy private life. You never drank much more than the rest of us did; you just let your mask slip more. But in your case, it's smartest to remove the booze as an issue altogether. At least now when you're making bad decisions, you'll be doing it with a clear head. And it could save you a testicle or two when that she-devil you married decides to wield the lawyers: *My client has tried everything, your honor* . . . (And yes, I realize she's even harder work when you're sober.)

It's expected of a man to get drunk in his twenties, it's accepted of him in his thirties, but by the time he hits his forties, like you, Monty, it's just sad. And you're far too smart a guy for us to be feeling sorry for you. So it's coffee only for all of us at the cards from now on, by the way. Tommy insisted.

Call into the hospital on Friday evening and we'll get a chat.

Dave

Police Headquarters, Derry

Dear Mr Schumann

A suspect in the murder of John-Joe McGownie and in the attempted murder of Ellie McGinlay, Barry Bruskin, aka Barry Bang Bang, was stopped by officers close to the Mountrose Road border crossing with Donegal last night.

He was held on a traffic violation (faulty brake light) for ten minutes and then released. His whereabouts are currently unknown, but it is believed he returned across the border.

Yours sincerely
Edward O'Conway, Chief Superintendent

COVER NOTE

HFC

Dave

What can I say? Pair of bloody amateurs. Traffic cops – they didn't know who they had and they spooked him right back into his burrow.

You can have all the planning in the world, but you should never underestimate a copper's ability to fuck everything up. Sincere, sincere apologies.

Ed

Altnagelvin Hospital, Derry

Dear Pop

I've believed all my life that it is possible to win at any game by playing fairly and by being smarter and more patient than your opponent. You taught me that. It doesn't matter how dirty someone gets; if you resort to their tactics you become as bad as they are. Or as you always advise: "Never get involved in a stink fight with a skunk."

Now, though, I'm not so sure. I'm looking over at Ellie's corpse-white face, wondering if she'll ever open her eyes again and thinking that the normal rules of engagement aren't doing us any good this time. The people who poisoned her and Mary McDarragh and Peggy O'Whelan, and indeed who shot John-Joe McGownie, are just too clever for due process. And I can't see how we can beat them fairly.

In saying that, the one abiding reason I never resorted to foul tactics, whether in basketball, politics or journalism, was much more self-serving and had little or nothing to do with morality. The simple truth? I was never any good at cheating; and any time I did it, I got caught. And now, in this never-private new world, where your every sordid misdeed can be replayed a thousand times on any home computer and your every sordid thought can be retraced by Google, I know for certain that it's pointless to try and dupe the camera.

I never liked it much either when my team mates got involved in the rough stuff. It puts the rest of the group at risk. I remember one post-game row in the BU dressing rooms after we won by dint of a very sneaky

Marty Kirk foul in center court. I refused to shake his hand – and he never forgave me for it.

All of which brings me to my point. Before I left for the hospital tonight, I rang Chris to ask if Chad could have a look at a number of computers at Whitman House which have been infected with a magnificently pornographic virus. But she told me, in a surprised voice (that suggested I should know better), that Chad was 'helping out' in the interrogation.

"What interrogation?" I asked, confused.

"The Bruskin one," she retorted.

And she then stopped dead and sucked in air, suddenly aware that she'd given the game away. Shit! The envoy wasn't supposed to know.

I pressed her as to where they were holding him – ordered her, pleaded with her even – but she had gone to that polite-but-firm non-answering place where they teach CEOs to go as soon as they become CEOs and face difficult questions on a daily basis.

The scariest part is I don't even know who's working with Chad on this one. I'm assuming at least one of my closest friends is involved, but the beauty is . . . I'll never know. Ed, I would think, would have to be there – though it hurts me that he could have lied so blatantly about Bruskin's escape. And Tommy is so prescient I would imagine that Chad would want him in as well. Tommy, as his own niece disclosed, used to serve as an 'honest observer' at in-house paramilitary trials during the bad old days here. (Though less sympathetic individuals have claimed his role was more that of a judge.)

The real lesson for me in this is that Chad Scarpa has as much, if not more, authority in this neck of the woods as I do. And it doesn't derive from his seventy-note-a-year paycheck as head doorman at Dunsuffrin.

I've long suspected his dual role, but protocol demands that I never comment on it, or even allude to it. He had the run of the consulate here, long before I arrived. Suffice to say, Chad's security clearance is so high that he was one of only three personnel permitted to work on the installation of the new computer suite at Mountrose PSNI Barracks. Indeed, Chris has regularly 'sublet' him out to do similar jobs at police stations, army garrisons, universities and colleges right across the island. He's also installed networks in at least two major newspapers I know of. So, in short, there isn't a piece of worthwhile intelligence that goes into a computer anywhere in Ireland that Chad can't access if he needs to. Another reason I find myself resorting to pen and ink more and more. Chad, of course, never writes anything down.

For all my contact with Chad, I've never been able to get a bead on his moral compass. He exudes this all-American aura of honor and fair play, loves his mother and goes to church on Sunday. But recently, I'm sensing what you might call an Old Testament approach to perceived enemies. And now, he has single-handedly tracked down a brutal child killer and, from what I understand, he feels he's got no option but to put him to the sword. All the while protecting me.

I fear for Bruskin, I really do. But that's not my main problem. Nor is the fact that Chad Scarpa is ultimately doing all this in my name, albeit beneath seven layers of deniability. No. My real difficulty is that I'm going to be perfectly happy to live on, knowing what happened and keeping my mouth shut about it. As ultimately, the world will have been corrected.

Tommy is due back in an hour to relieve me – he's got the overnight shift, so I'll know more then. He'll not even have to say a word; it'll be written all over his face. He's like me in that – he'll never make a professional poker player.

I'll talk to you on Sunday.

So long and slán
Your loving son
David

Police Headquarters, Derry

Dear Mr Schumann

Following searches at a number of addresses in Mountrose today, police have recovered 20,000 Ecstasy tablets and four kilos of cannabis resin, which we understand were being 'stockpiled' for the forthcoming festival.

Other confidential information I am privy to suggests that this seizure represents only a small percentage of the total cache destined for the town in the run-up to next month's festival.

I am formally requesting that you now use your influence to postpone the festival; otherwise, the PSNI will be forced to seek its cancellation through the courts.

Further to your other inquiry, police have had no reports of either a kidnapping or a missing person in the Mountrose area over the past two weeks. It is possible, if not likely, that the individual concerned has travelled abroad on business.

Yours sincerely
Edward O'Conway, Chief Superintendent

COVER NOTE

HFC

Christ, Dave, would you stop playing silly buggers and weigh in behind your own men? Thanks to our private interview with our mutual friend, we've now more data about the pipeline and distributors than we'd have got with two years' solid surveillance. And we've also scored our third major seizure in the past two months.

Let me also assure you that absolutely no harm has come to the suspect. Rather, he has since been the subject of a private extradition order to another jurisdiction, where he will answer questions about a number of terrorist atrocities. We're not the people who bury bodies in the bogs, Dave.

And yes, I know it'll cost you a small bundle to call off the gig at this late stage – but if it goes ahead, you might as well just take that same bundle of cash and hand it over to the Gallowgate Mafia, or whatever the Scottish connection call themselves.

I'll talk to you at the hospital later this evening. In the meantime, say nothing to Tommy. This is not his affair.

Ed

Liars' Row, Dunavady

HFC

Dave

Just back at the office to clear the desk and picked up your message. I'm afraid I can't help.

Ed's right. You can end this thing right now by calling off the concert. I'll even be the bad guy, if you need me to, by launching a legal challenge to it in a private capacity – to take the heat off you. The press will lap it up: 'Distraught relative of a near-dead drugs victim' et cetera, et cetera. A nod from you and it'll sail right through the court.

I don't know who's giving him his lines at the moment (I'm obviously better off not knowing), but Ed's convinced that this week's haul is only the sugar on the doughnut. So do the right thing, Dave, and close the damn coffee shop.

And yes, I know Chris will pout a bit, but you've only got to look at her for a couple more weeks. Maybe Chad might talk some sense into her when he gets back from his conference in Riga.

Ed, by the way, can't do the late shift tomorrow at the hospital; any chance you could fill in? If I miss another night's sleep, I'm at serious risk of standing up in court and telling the truth about my clients.

Yours in exhaustion
Tommy

Town Hall, Mountrose

HFC

Dave

Chris has been telling me you're under pressure to call off the concert. She is not a happy bunny at all and is already ruing her decision to let you out of the car boot on the night of your breaking-up party. (Great concept. But for the record, Clooney and Lopez were fully dressed.)

Seriously, it was a real achievement for Chris to land the Dirty Big Dogs, and Dunsuffrin have invested a significant amount of their own money in the festival and in the preparations for the vice-presidential visit. I appreciate her concern that we risk painting Mountrose as some sort of drugs capital if we shut it down now, when in fact it's one of the safest places on the planet.

But I also know the politics of this, though – and the repercussions for the town if the festival goes wrong. So I do think you're going to have to cave to Ed eventually and postpone the thing at the very least. But given the very delicate talks we're still in with inward investors, it would be useful to me if you could delay any decision for another week, possibly eight days at most. This would also give you a chance to hang the whole debacle on the heads of the Dirty Big Dogs, who, let's be honest about it, deserve most of the blame anyway. (*Tune in and burn out* – Jeez, they should just go ahead and give away free spliffs with every CD.)

A delay would also give Chris time to organise an alternative – something a little less contentious – maybe an opera event, or something else that only boring, non-drug-taking punters would travel to watch.

Ed said he could live with you holding back an official announcement as long as he had your word it was coming soon. He got very good press out of the recent seizures, and there's the real possibility he could snare another batch or two, given some luck and a few extra days. From what I hear, they broke their mole so badly, he'll never appear in these parts again – not even as a very, very old man. (And as the poet said, small fucking odds, Joxer.)

Coincidentally, Bruskin has just disappeared off the face of the earth. Who'd have thunk he'd run away, eh? And has anyone seen Chad Scarpa this week? (Ha, ha.)

Ed was telling me that Nero has been sighted by our friends in Donegal, where he's looking for bar work. But they're confident he'll return home. His father has only a day or two left, tops, and he'll have to come to say goodbye. The nature of that beast is always family first. There was talk that Nero's sister might transport the father by car over to Donegal Town earlier in the week to see the son. But the doctor warned her not to move him or he'd pretty much die on the spot.

You could argue that with Nero and Bang Bang gone, the concert could go ahead unimpeded. And with Darkly likely to be in custody for another week or so, the network is all but shut down.

It's also just possible that Ed has done a completely thorough job in containing our problem and that the Dirty Big Dogs could wind up headlining in the new, drug-free capital of Ireland. Yet another reason to postpone your decision.

All I'm asking is that you give us a bit of breathing space. I assure you I'll respect whatever decision you reach.

May you always have the courage to change the things you can.

Your friend
Monty

Whitman House, Derry

HFC

Tommy

Enclosed find a copy of Monty's latest memo, as promised. Reading between the lines, the butcher has the knife all sharpened up and Monty's poor little scrotum is on the chopping block. He's playing it so well, too; his argument is plausible enough to be convincing, but it's just a shade too sincere to ring true.

They've got to him – whoever 'they' are. For my money, I'd be pretty certain Darkly has sent out the warning via Kitty O. They must reckon that if I leave the decision to cancel too late, the big guns in Belfast will override me and let the concert go ahead. Which also means the bad guys have already got some sort of delivery strategy in place.

I'm reluctant to clue Ed or Chad in just yet, as the typical copper strategy is always to break the weakest link, which in this case will be Monty. And I'm damned if I'm going to put one of my closest friends through fifteen rounds of Hide the Electric Cattle Prod just because he's a sucker for good-looking women.

Let's face it: this is one area where I have little or no moral high ground.

Just on that topic, Chris called in to visit Ellie tonight, fair play to her, and leave in another book. The duty nurse reckons Chris is still hankering after me, and will be changing her travel plans, sure as dogs have fleas. But I don't think so. And the truth is, Tommy, I don't want her to, either.

I've finally worked out that you can't truly love someone until you've seen them at their most vulnerable. And Chris, for all her gorgeous glamour, is pretty much bullet proof. I'd swap a lifetime with her in the fast lane for these past couple of weeks spent keeping guard over Sleeping Beauty.

And just so you know, I'll be staying here for as long as it takes. But sure you knew that anyway.

Your friend
Dave

Whitman House, Derry

CONFIDENTIAL

Cc
Mayor Montgomery Boyce, Mountrose Town Hall
US Ambassador, London

Dear Chief Superintendent O'Conway

I would like to put you on notice that I intend to make an announcement in one week's time, cancelling the rock-music element of the Mountrose Festival.

I have taken the decision in light of the recent substantial drugs seizures – and intelligence you and other agencies have accrued – which suggests the event, in its current form, could present a danger to public safety.

Over the next week I will be meeting with various groups to discuss incorporating other events into the festival schedule that would be more in keeping with the state visit.

I would respectfully ask that you NOT release this information to anyone until our new arrangements are in place.

Yours sincerely
David Schumann

COVER NOTE

HFC

Ed

For all sorts of reasons, I need a week's grace before I say anything.

First off, I haven't seen Chris so mad since I confused her edible undies with an $800 pair of hand-spun silk panties (fill in the blanks yourself). I offered to help her with standing down the Dirty Big Dogs, but she insists on doing it personally. I was even prepared to get the Brits to pull their singer's visa on the grounds he has more strikes against him than a one-armed little-leaguer. But she just told me to go stick it in a light socket, and that she'd sort out the mess herself.

Monty also needs time to get his stories in a row. He'll be happy enough, though, if we land the Three Tenors, as it'll have all the cultural kudos of a rockfest without any of the attendant looting and pillaging. For the minute, though, he's giving me the petted lip and silent treatment.

As if that all weren't enough, Chad Scarpa is ticked off as well – in as much as Chad can be ticked off about anything – but only because he didn't close down the pipeline in time. He's asked me to meet him to discuss a possible compromise that'd allow him (and Chris, I suspect) to save a little face. So I'll do that, too, as a matter of courtesy. But I'll leave it as close to the announcement as possible so that there's no chance he can talk me round.

The bottom line, Ed, is that while we managed to stop Darkly, Bruskin and Nero, we couldn't – and were never going to – shut down the rest of the world. And unfortunately, the rest of the world was intending to descend on Mountrose next month. Unless we shut down Mountrose. And that, unfortunately, is what we were reduced to doing.

See you tomorrow for the night shift at the hospital.

Dave

chad@dunsuffrin.net

<u>URGENT</u>

Dave

Give me a bell, pronto.

C

schumann@derryconsulate.com

<u>URGENT</u>

Chad

Pick up your damn phone.

D

Whitman House, Derry

<u>URGENT</u>

Tommy

We have the breakthrough! Nero's handed himself in to Chad at the plant. It was the father's dying wish for the son to go straight. And as I'm rapidly discovering, there's no more powerful agent on this planet than Catholic guilt. (Or non-monetary agent, at least.)

Nero's coughing to everything but better again, is handing us Darkly on a plate. He says Darkly set up the Glasgow connection through old racing buddies of his brother, who was a jockey over there.

Darkly also paid Bang Bang Bruskin for the McGownie shooting. Apparently poor John-Joe had been shaving his percentage, and it was important to set an example for the others.

Bruskin, as we thought, was Ellie's meet the night she got spiked. And Nero admitted that he gave Bang Bang the MDMA solution for her drink. The plan, however, was never to kill her, just get her to embarrass herself and then take a few compromising pictures. (Better to own a cow you can milk, as you always say.) But despite all the warnings, Bang Bang used far too much of the juice.

Chad reckons it might be possible to use what Nero's told him to set a trap for the Glasgow gang, but he's advising against bringing in the police at this stage – on the grounds that, other than Ed, none of them knows a damn what they're doing.

I'm heading over to Dunsuffrin now; Chad's going to debrief Chris, Monty and myself, after which I'll come and fill you in at the hospital.

At last, we're sucking diesel!

Dave

bowtie@dunavady.net

TOP PRIORITY

Ed

Ellie's just come round – head clear as Derry crystal, thank God. We need to find Dave. He's somewhere in Mountrose but his iPhone and car phone are both off. I think we have a problem. A serious problem. Get into your car this minute, turn on your mobile and I'll give you the gen.

TB

Dunsuffrin Plant, Mountrose

Dear Pop

I'm not sure this will ever reach you, but if it doesn't, you can be sure I'm dead. And yes, I realize that makes no sense at all – particularly since, even if you do get to read it, there is a good chance I'm not feeling too healthy, either.

I've very little time, so I'll cut to the chase. It was Monty who inadvertently gave it away.

Chris and he were already waiting in Chad's office when I arrived. Nero, I was informed, was in a locked room three doors down writing out his confession.

As soon as I sat down, Chad began priming us with some background about Nero and company – drug running, stabbings, beatings etc. Awful stuff. Very bad people. Chad was stressing that, because of his various contacts, his information was Grade One. He couldn't miss the opportunity to let us know who he was without actually saying it. Again.

Then Monty, the little kiss-ass, announced, just to show how connected he is, that Chad had actually installed the computer suite in the Derry police station – and that he could read every piece of data processed by the PSNI in the entire North West. And Chad, of course, nodded his head in solemn agreement.

And it was at that moment the scales started falling from my eyes. They'd been spinning Monty a slightly different line from me. They'd told me that Chad had rigged out *Mountrose*. But Ed had previously disclosed to me that it was his own two nephews – both IT specialists with the Guards – who'd got the contract to computerize the Derry station, just before Chad moved to Derry. So what Chad (or Chris) had told Monty was a lie. A small lie. But a lie is a lie – and a liar is a liar, just the same.

Then, almost immediately, the second lie rang home in my head. Chad once boasted to me that he'd installed the security systems in all of Darkly Barkley's pubs and clubs – including the Pink Paradise. And now here I was in Chad's office, and he was bragging that every system he ever installed is automatically routed to his own server here at Dunsuffrin, before it's even saved onto in-house PCs. Which means, of course, Chad had the footage of Ellie all along – and whoever poisoned her.

As I continued to listen to Chad listing Nero's sins, I was suddenly struck by the silence in the room. Normally, the entire plant is throbbing, even at weekends; they work a three-shift day, seven days a week.

"Very quiet today," I said to Chris.

"Surprised you never noticed it before," she smiled. "We insulated the top floor here from all the factory noise. And the entire administration department has been given a half-day for exceeding their targets."

Chad smiled over benevolently at his kind boss as if to say you could have given me the day off as well, and scratched his ankle absentmindedly. But as he did, his trouser leg rode up slightly and I spied the St Andrew's Cross tattoo on his big brown calf.

And it was then I knew. If I didn't go immediately, I might never get out of the room.

I thought the bottom was going to fall out of my stomach. But while I still had the nerve, I stood up like I was in charge and announced that – after all this excitement – I needed a quick restroom break and that we'd reconvene in two minutes. Chris nodded to Chad it was okay and I made for the door.

As soon as I left the office, I just kept going down stairs and along empty corridors until I found this open supply closet. All the exit doors are locked tight, and my damn cell phone's in the car. So it's down to pen and paper, I'm afraid. Not how I expected to be saying my goodbyes, but you take what you get.

I have no idea what their plan is, but I do know they'll do anything to make this concert happen. Including, I suspect, taking out a US envoy. They have too much invested in it. After all, they're making the drugs here – just as you predicted they were, Pop – and they've been doing it since day one. Scotland, Derry, the chemist van and the Fat Teddy bag switch were all red herrings to keep the rest of us so distracted we couldn't spot the big lie.

And as for the Dunsuffrin security being so tight you couldn't get an asthma inhaler inside? What a line. I should never have forgotten my Latin: *Quis custodiet ipsos custodes*? Who will police the police themselves?

And Chris? How could I have been so dumb? A smoking-hot Delilah in a pair of Jimmy Choo pumps. She played me like a Steinway piano. My God, the only one who spotted her was a seventy-one-year-old dementia patient. I swear, if I ever get out of this, I'm going to start doing some of my thinking with my brain.

I can hear the factory alarm sounding now and I'm afraid it might be tolling for me, Pop. I'm going to hide this note inside a box of computer paper, in the hope that it someday might surface into the right hands.

I love you, Pop – and I love Mom, too. Always have. Always will.

So long and slán
Your loving son
David

Police Headquarters, Derry

CONFIDENTIAL

Dear Mr McGinlay

As you are aware, the three individuals questioned about yesterday's unfortunate incident at the Dunsuffrin Plant in Mountrose were released immediately and without charge.

There is absolutely no evidence to support claims that the fire at the new manufacturing wing, in which Mr O'Neary died, was started by anyone other than the dead man himself. It is public knowledge that the deceased had recently made threats against both the factory's CEO and a number of its managers.

Twenty assorted offices and an 8,000-square-foot shop floor, plus a substantial quantity of what was termed 'raw product' being stored there, were totally destroyed.

Dunsuffrin International, however, have already issued a statement from their Anchorage HQ that they will not allow this one-off incident to spoil their otherwise excellent relationship with Ireland.

Yours sincerely
Edward O'Conway, Chief Superintendent

COVER NOTE

HFC

Tommy

Do you remember the scene in *Lethal Weapon II* when the evil bastard South African minister holds up his wallet with a grin and demands 'diplomatic immunity'? I never cheered as much as when Danny Glover revoked his status and shot him between the eyes. And now I know why. Because in the real world, that can never happen.

The fire was already well alight by the time I got to the plant. They'd probably primed (or bribed) one of the nurses to tip them off if Ellie woke up and they'd their contingency plan ready. All Chad had to do was strike a match, and the lab – and a couple of million dollars' worth of MDMA – went up like a bag of hay.

Nero's body was soaked in some sort of accelerant – petrol, I'd guess – and was burnt so badly that no pathologist could ever tell if he died from smoke inhalation, burns or a crack on the head before he was tossed into the fire. Which, of course, was the whole point. He must have spilled it over himself when he was starting the blaze.

The two Yanks were standing talking animatedly with Monty outside the burning wing when I arrived. Chad had already ordered all the other staff off the site '"for their own safety", and they were filing out in their droves as I made my way in.

I knew by the time I reached the trio that I'd lost. That there would be no investigation. No inquiry. No post mortem for Nero. Nothing beyond the few cursory inquiries I would make before buying the official line. As given to me by Chad.

So for the sake of form, I pointed down towards the maintenance shed, which I knew to be empty, and told the three of them to follow me there so we could clarify a couple of details.

Chad did his best not to smirk as he led the way. He'd tied it all up neater than a Sunday hat. Monty, the snake, was already praising Chad's bravery in trying to save poor, misunderstood Nero. And Chris looked like a woman whose biggest problem in the world was choosing which brand of sun cream she'd be taking with her for her big new job in Fort Lauderdale.

Inside the hut, they fed me their bullshit for a few minutes, and I threw out two or three tame questions. The only time they looked rattled was at the end when I asked Chad straight out what had happened the body wire he was supposed to have given Ellie for her meeting with Bruskin. I studied his face as he considered lying, then watched him weigh up the fact he was going back to the US in a week's time anyway and couldn't care less. So I should have known what was coming next.

"Diplomatic immunity," he grinned at me.

And it was then I heard Dave's voice at the door behind me: "What about Mary McDarragh, Ed? And Peggy O'Whelan? And John-Joe McGownie? Are you going to let him away with that . . . just because he spends a little money here?"

I looked back towards the door. Dave was a sight: face creased with dirt, hair all mussed up and his crisp white shirt streaked with soot and grime.

Chad glanced over at him and laughed. "So what are *you* going to do, big shot? Tattle on me? I already told this cop jock, I've got diplomatic immunity. And just in case you've forgotten, I know where all your bodies are buried, too."

And he was right. He did.

Chad stood up and began walking purposefully to the door. This meeting was over.

But at that moment, Dave caught my eye and lowered his chin very slightly. It's that selfsame nod he gives me at cards every week when he wants to tell me that Monty's bluffing. And I knew instinctively what he wanted.

You see, in the real world, if you go around shooting diplomats between the eyes, you're going to spend the rest of your life in jail – or, maybe in my case, on the late-night loony desk in Dunavady. Which, I assure you, is even worse.

So instead, I did what Dave, I, and, indeed, you, should have done the very first day we met Chad Scarpa. I pulled out my service revolver and shot him in the arse.

"Sorry about that," I said to the room. "I thought I saw someone trying to flee the building. I must have been mistaken."

"You were right," agreed Dave. "I thought I saw someone, too."

Chris and Monty didn't move as I kept my gun trained on Chad. He looked up at me from the floor with all the venom of a man who's just struck a very bad deal but one he's going to have to live with. Or more pertinently, perhaps, like a man who's going to walk with a limp for about a year and then carry a rubber ring to the toilet for the rest of his life.

"Five years in Anchorage for you, Chris," continued Dave, a judge handing down a sentence. "No access to the main Forty-Eight, either. You always said Dunsuffrin would kill to have you back at HQ. And now you're going.

"Monty, you're out as mayor. Blame your family commitments. Any messing from either of you, and honest to God, we'll disappear you quicker than Chad did Bang Bang. You understand?"

They both nodded their heads silently.

"Chad," Dave went on, "if you ever poke your head up in Ireland again, I promise you, that hole in your ass is going to get a matching pair . . . only it'll be Darragh McDarragh performing the honours with his shotgun. And he'll be standing a lot closer. You understand?"

Chad closed his eyes.

And with that, it was over. A shitty result all round. And like all good compromises, everyone was mad.

But for the first time since I've known him, I realised what Dave is doing here. I've often said, Tommy, that you're the only person I know who sees the whole picture. Dave, however, is the guy who directs it.

Ed

Tommy Bowtie writes:

It was a bad deal, no doubt, but while I've thought about it a thousand times since, I could never concoct a better one. Dave had put it together in the thirty seconds it took him from breaking out of a burning building, which the bastards had locked, to confronting them at the maintenance shed.

Our problem was that we were all complicit at different stages of the lie – as Chad had reminded us. We couldn't kill him, because we didn't know whom he'd been talking to, and we couldn't arrest Chris or, sure as shooting, they'd end up shutting down the biggest single factory in this part of the island. If it had been me, I might have shot her in the backside as well. After all, she was the honey that let us swallow all the horseshit.

They were just so damned smart, the two of them. Smart enough to send us chasing countless false trails while they built their little empire. Smart enough to convince the US government to pay top dollar for a festival where they could then peddle their drugs. Smart enough to try to burn Dave alive before he'd called off the gig. And smart enough to dump Nero's body into the blaze to put him in the frame for it. And ultimately, what saved them is that they were smart enough never to write anything down. Not ever.

Ed was wrong about one thing, though. About me seeing the full picture. As I explained to him later, I'd spent so long believing I saw the picture, I missed what was staring me in the face. I had bought into the big lie, just like everyone else.

MAY
♥

CEO's Office
Zonk-Zonk Industries, Boston

Cc
US Consul, Belfast, US Ambassador, Dublin
US Ambassador, London

Dear Mr Schumann

Further to our recent discussions, I would like to confirm, officially, that Zonk-Zonk Industries now intends to establish its European headquarters in Mountrose, County Londonderry, and *not* in Belfast as was prematurely reported in sections of the Irish media.

We will gladly avail of your most generous offer to base the new plant on the fifteen-acre site to the east of the town, recently gifted to you by Mr D Barkley for development purposes. The plant will house an R&D department, a manufacturing division and the previously agreed medical-packaging facility along with a substantial administration block. In all, we envisage employing 1,200 people from the North West of Ireland in Mountrose.

We would like to pay tribute to both yourself and Mr Barkley for the honest and informative manner in which you presented your case for Mountrose. And we would also like to put on record our appreciation for the complete confidentiality you showed throughout the negotiating process.

Yours sincerely
Eric Zweithand, Chief Executive Officer

Whitman House, Derry

Dear Pop

It was a risky decision to cancel both the visit and the festival, but I think you're right that it would have been riskier again to let them go ahead. Just in case we'd left an unexploded mine somewhere. It was the easiest thing in the world to hang it on the Dirty Big Dogs, too – idiots thought they could hide a pound-and-a-half of weed inside a loudspeaker. Do they think none of us ever lived in a college dorm?

We gave the punters precisely one whole day to bitch about having no circus before we showered them with bread. (Once again, thank you, Juvenal. That Latin minor was money well spent.) The news of Zonk-Zonk's arrival completely reset the agenda, with all of Ireland hailing Mountrose as Europe's new pharmaceutical capital – or Diazepam Valley, as the locals now call it. Darkly's 'gift' of the land sealed the deal; although, between ourselves, he was also obliged to match Belfast's original half-mill sweetener to big Eric. And yes, in doing so, Barkley managed to buy himself down from ten years with no parole to a twenty-four-month sabbatical at a country-club jail. But he'll never have another buddy like Chad Scarpa to help him when he gets out.

Belfast were extremely pissed at Zonk-Zonk's *volte face* – no-one had ever stolen jobs back from them before. So much so that the consulate was forced to ban me from all trade missions for a year. Not that it matters, as I think we've just witnessed the last flurry of US outsourcing for a few years . . . until the recession lifts.

The State Department are a little ticked off at me as well. Chad Scarpa had been a first-class servant to them here before he got bored, and they're not at all happy he's out of commission, albeit temporarily. But they accept that Ed O'Conway, and indeed Tommy Bowtie, would have blown the whistle on the factory-within-a-factory if I hadn't taken some action. And that would have caused an international incident. So Chad's going to have to take it on the chin, so to speak, even if the under-secretary did use the term "grossly disproportionate" four times during his secure video call to me.

As a punishment, they've told me they're refusing to transfer me for the term of the Administration, so denying me permanent access to my 'girlfriend', who's now back in Alaska. Not sure who dreamt up that one, but I think the Veep might have had a hand in it, as it couldn't suit me any better.

Tommy has clued in Ellie on most of what transpired, as he figures it's the only way to stop her asking awkward questions. He left out the part where I took Ed's gun and shot Chad in the ass, of course. He doesn't want her thinking she's involved with a card-carrying sadist. And anyway, Ed's made it clear he's happy to carry the can for the shooting – he even wrote it down in a private note to Tommy, so he could show it to Ellie.

The poker starts again on Saturday night. Mary Slavin, the *Derry Standard* editor, is going to take Monty's chair. Monty, in retrospect, was right to take a fresh start, and I'm sure he'll make a great head of marketing for Dunsuffrin in Anchorage. The guy is the archetypal Public Relations pro: a born liar, with no loyalties, no scruples, and no tells. And yet, for all his treachery, he's one of the most charming men I've ever met. He'll go far . . . and I'll miss him.

Ellie has made a full recovery, although she's still not allowed to drink alcohol until her pee returns to a socially acceptable color. We've our first official date tonight, but she's already warned me that it doesn't matter if I did spend a month reading to her in hospital, I'm still getting nothing under her sweater. Rules are rules. I told her I'd already given her a dozen bed baths, so I know I'm not missing much anyway . . .

This one is going to be really special, Pop. She challenges me, needles me, motivates me and irritates me. Even scares me a little. But, as you once said, for all that, she makes me want to try harder.

And there's something else I've noticed: the way she looks at me. I hate to be sappy about it, but it reminds me of the way Mom looks at you. And Old Mommy looked at Old Poppy. And no-one, but no-one has ever looked at me like that before.

Anyhow, you'll be able to tell all this for yourself when you come visit next month. But in the meantime, tell Mom from me that she'll probably have redheaded grandchildren after all. God bless her anti-Irish heart!

So long and slán
Your loving son
David

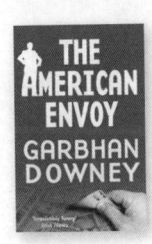

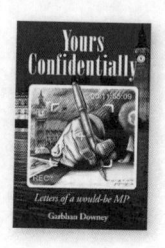

Praise for Garbhan Downey's Work

War of the Blue Roses (2009)

Sunday Tribune: Inventive, with a sharp sense of the ridiculous.

Ulster Tatler: It shocks you one minute, has you laughing out loud the next, and ultimately is impossible to put down. (Book of the Month, September 2009)

Irish Mail on Sunday: Acidic, humorous – he is an expert at the narrative rabbit punch.

Derry Journal: Fast-moving, dazzlingly clever and often laugh-out-loud funny. It would make a great film script. A new peak – a personal best.

Londonderry Sentinel: I actually had to put the book down because the tears were running down my face.

Andersonstown News: If there is any justice in the literary world, this will be the book that raises Garbhan Downey's profile to its full potential.

Culture NI: Lashings of spying, killing and romance – a thrilling and intelligent send-up of global politics.

Local Women: This rollicking satire is sure to stir your political consciousness and prompt many a belly-laugh.

Hughes & Hughes: Book of the Month, August 2009.

Yours Confidentially (2008)

Philadelphia Inquirer: Selected as one of the newspaper's top seven International Crime Fiction books of 2008.

Fortnight: Rave I shall about Garbhan Downey! The dealing of his Dunavady constituency makes Jeffrey Archer's Westminster wranglings looks positively puerile. My book of the year is *Yours Confidentially: Letters of a would-be MP*.

Irish Mail on Sunday: Sharp, witty and succinct. All I say is, Vote Downey.

Verbal: Downey manages to tell a tale with a verve and effortless style that knocked my socks off. I'm telling you right now, it's the funniest book I've read this year. And I read a lot.

Derry Journal: It's Garbhan Downey at his very best, with cruel one-liners packed onto every page.

Londonderry Sentinel: Downey has now firmly established himself as a genuinely fine exponent of the political novel genre.

Running Mates (2007)

Irish News: Irresistibly funny. A wickedly sharp and often hilarious portrayal of the crookery that takes place behind closed doors in the run-up to an election.

Irish Independent: Downey's latest offering is unashamedly creating a new kind of genre – the Irish cross-border political thriller. Its rapid-fire pace, intriguing twists, high body count and brilliant dialogue make it a really exciting read and a worthy addition to the ever-growing list of classy Irish crime novels.

Sunday Business Post: Fast-paced, outlandish and funny.

Irish Mail on Sunday: This blackly humorous romp fizzes with dark wit and has a razor-sharp edge.

New York Irish Voice: He's a bit of a one is Garbhan Downey. In his new novel, a fast-paced satire of Irish politics and political life, thinly veiled Irish public figures are given the full treatment … Downey has a talent for writing vivid dialogue in the Irish vernacular that makes this outrageous caper work on its own terms.

News Letter: A really good book … a brilliantly plotted and written comedy romp through a tremendously corrupt race for the Irish presidency.

Ulster Herald: His style captures the fly-boy humour and wise-cracking lack of deference of his Derry City home. Yet it is his knowledge of what former Irish President Erskine Childers once described longingly as the 'cut and thrust' of Irish party politics that gives *Running Mates* its surprising authenticity. This work of fiction will amuse and inform anybody with even an inkling of interest in Irish politics in a new era. This is one to savour.

Alternative Ulster: Fictional gold … a hilarious romp through affairs of state.

Kenny's Books, Ireland (Fiction Book of the Month, July 2007): A roller-coaster tale – a good, cynical look at the Northern attitude towards the South and vice versa.

Off Broadway (2005)

Sunday World: A belly-laugh-on-every-page collection of short stories which will shoot to the top of the shoplifters' book-of-the-week almost overnight.

Modern Woman: A master stylist ... damnit, you can almost taste the steam off the pages.

Ireland on Sunday: Nothing is sacred ... many laugh-out-loud moments.

Daily Ireland: A nail-biting read. It's sharp, cynical, often caustic, but always enjoyable.

Woman's Way: A viciously funny look at the rise of crookery and roguery in Ireland since the ceasefires.

Derry Journal: An instant hit ... from the smoking gun to the smoking suitcase, *Off Broadway* gives the reader an insight into what is really going on all over the post-ceasefire North.

Private Diary of a Suspended MLA (2004)

Sunday Times: The best Northern Ireland political novel of the century.

Irish News: If there is anything good that came out of the suspension of the Assembly, it has to be the idea which inspired Garbhan Downey to write *Private Diary of a Suspended MLA*.

Sunday Tribune: A hilarious romp.

Belfast Telegraph: A gem ... this new author is eagle eyed and as sharp as a lance.

Hot Press: Rude'n'racy ... gleefully sends up the Northern political process.

Sunday Journal: By the time I had read the second paragraph, I knew it was going to be a *tour de force*.

Derry News: Expect a literary smack in the mouth.